THE DIVINE CHRONICLES
IMMORTAL
Book 4

ROB RADCLIFFE

Copyright © 2025 Rob Radcliffe 2025
The right of Rob Radcliffe to be identified as the author of this work has been asserted by him in accordance with the Copyright, Designs and Patents Act 1988.
All rights reserved. No part of this publication may be reproduced, stored in or introduced into a retrieval system, or transmitted, in any form, or by any means (electronic, mechanical, photocopying, recording or otherwise) without the prior written permission of the publisher. Any person who does any unauthorized act in relation to this publication may be liable to criminal prosecution and civil claims for damages.

Published By Radcliffe Press

For those who wonder, "What if…"

Also By Rob Radcliffe...

The Divine Chronicles...

MESSIAH - *Prequel*

GUARDIAN - I

DIVINE - II

HEALER - III

IMMORTAL - IV

RECKONING - V

Legends Of Athea...

ONCE UPON A TIDE

THE LOST BOY *(Coming Soon)*

The Reluctant Writer Series...

UNLEASHED

The Lad-Lit series...

THE RACE - *Prequel*

MEAT MARKET

ESCORTING ERIC

BARMAN

THE OTHER SIDE

TINDERED

CHECKING OUT

The Windfall Series…

LUCKY MAN

LADY LUCK

LUCK OF THE DRAW

www.robradcliffe.com

THE DIVINE CHRONICLES

IMMORTAL

A MEMOIR

ROB RADCLIFFE

Prologue

A NEW DAWN

It is widely accepted these days that man evolved from apes, and that if we traced our ancestry back through the ages all of man and today's apes would arrive at one being, the common ancestor. Slowly through time our mother ape's offspring branched out into many different species, but it was the evolution of man which would shape the world in which we now live. Indeed it was man who conquered the earth.

Although hard to imagine the early days, through thousands and then millions of years, mankind's path spewed off from that of the apes, creating new species. Man evolved from Homo-habilis to Homo-erectus, and then finally to the Homo-sapiens. At each point along this journey man changed, his brain growing larger and with it he learned new tricks to hedge his chances of survival on the earth. From fashioning tools to help him hunt, the discovery of fire, creating shelter and then communities, agriculture, religion, war, construction, industry, and technology, man's destiny as the planet's dominant species has spiralled him to the top of the food chain where he has remained indefinitely. The survival of the species was down to their larger brains which, in turn, have guaranteed them their mantel.

Let us go back for a moment, back to our mother ape. While we moved on through the ages her and her species died out, but we were not alone on this journey. Our cousins, whose ancestors and ours is the same, are today's Orang-utans, Gorillas, and Chimpanzees.

Over millions of years we all divided and went our separate ways, and then our particular species split again, creating a sub-species. It is believed that around three hundred and fifty thousand years ago five separate species of human lived on the earth at the same time, for about seventy thousand years. It is believed also that these five 'brothers', Homo-erectus, Homo-ergaster, Homo-neanderthalensis, Homo-heidelbergensis, and Homo-rhodesiensis lived in different parts of the world, although whether they fought, lived separately in their own communities, or even cross bred with one another is unknown.

Now a new dawn is upon us.

Although I can tell you that evolution's new dawn has been rising for eight hundred years, I cannot begin to estimate when my kind and mankind's split.

Am I an ambassador for the next step in mankind's journey?

Is my kind a sub-species of the Homo-sapien?

Is the Homo-sapien's time coming to a close?

These are questions I cannot answer, and I know by writing this memoir I will be putting not only myself, but my entire species under threat.

History has shown me time and time again that Man exterminates what he does not understand and so fears. It would be nice to say that through time Man has evolved in himself and learned the true nature of his namesake humanity, but this would be untrue. He has simply modified his methods, through technology, of culling that which he does not understand.

Man will fear us and a new war will be fought, not for religion or politics, land or wealth, but for fear of us, the unknown, the Divine. And I fear we still number so few that we will be slaughtered instead of embraced.

A new dawn is upon us all, we are the Divine and we are amongst you…

Chapter One

A FAREWELL

If you could live forever would you want to?

Given the choice, I don't believe I would choose yes. To be immortal, to refuse to age, to be stuck, stagnant, while all around you the world changes. Why would anyone want that for themselves? To love many and watch them all die, the constant loss, the turmoil and grief forever eating away at you. No, given the choice I would not choose to be immortal. Given the choice I would have died many centuries ago having had my time. But you cannot chose this life, the never ending rollercoaster, any more than you can chose to be born in the first place.

I know I am not the only one out there, but we hide well in plain sight. There is no secret hand-shake or nod of the head for us to recognise each other. There is no clubhouse with exclusive membership where we might find sanctuary, we are alone in this world until we happen across another. We have time on our side though, that much is unmistakeable.

I step into the rain and look out over the rolling fields, battered suitcase in one hand and train ticket in the other.

'Can't I at least drive you down to the train station Doc? Look at it, you'll be soaked through before you reach the end of the driveway.'

I turn to Eric, my friend since the war, the first world war that is, and shake my head, 'I'm Scottish by birth Eric, there'd be something very wrong if I couldn't handle a wee shower like this.' Holding out my hand Eric shakes it and then pulls me into him for a hug.

'Just be sure to call when you've found a place, ok?'

I agree to his terms and then just before I turn back towards my uncertain journey, I hear young Alan call from inside the house.

'Uncle William, Uncle William wait a moment.'

Alan knocks Eric out of the doorway, out of breath from his run from the other side of the house.

'Watch yourself boy,' Eric mumbles as Alan jumps off the front step and into my arms.

'Are you sure you can't stay a little longer?'

I smile down at Eric's nephew, the lad is all grown up now at twenty-one years old and still it feels like only moments ago he was running around crying for milk.

'I'd love to but I tire of your uncle's belly-aching over who ate the last of the eggs each morning.'

Alan laughs, 'But we have chickens, there are always fresh eggs.'

Looking over Alan's shoulder at Eric, who rolls his eyes, I say, 'There, you see Eric, there are always more eggs.' I slap Alan on the shoulder and hug him tight, kissing his head, 'No, it is time for me to head out into the big old world once again. These past six months have been delightful staying here with you but I have a job posting at a University in the south teaching medicine, and I wouldn't want to let all those stuffy professors down now would I?'

I make a face and Alan grins. It has been many years since I have had a child, watched them grow up into adults and head out into the world to find their own path. Alan, and indeed his older brother Peter, I have known since their first gulps of air as I was stood with Eric and the boy's father in the waiting room, pacing erratically with both men.

'Perhaps I might visit you Uncle William, when you have settled yourself into your new home?'

'Absolutely Al. You must all come down and visit. Right, that's enough chit-chat, I'd never step from Chesterfield Manor's grounds if you men had your way. Have a pleasant night, I'm leaving.'

With that I turn on my heel and head out into the rain, whistling as I walk down the driveway towards the entrance gates.

'Stay safe Doc,' Eric calls back to me and I lift an arm to acknowledge his words.

Pulling open the entrance gate I look back up the hill at Chesterfield Manor. Through the driving rain I catch one last glimpse of Alan at the front door, still waving me off. I sigh. It is time to reinvent myself once again.

When you live forever, reinvention is something which is often called for. I use the word *often* but mortal man would not think so. Every twenty, thirty, sometimes even forty years, we must abandon the lives we have built and reinvent ourselves as someone else in a new town, in a new country even. I have lived for over seven hundred years and have reinvented myself fifteen times. I have all the relevant identification on my person.

Birth Certificate, Passport, Drivers Licence and also a letter of recommendation for employment from Harvard Medical school. Sometimes when taking up teaching positions in the past, I have really sold myself. I was, after all, John Warren in a previous life, professor of anatomy and surgery and one of the three founding faculty members of the institute whose recommendation letter is in my pocket. This time around though, I am not pursuing a career, merely a standing in the community where people will not ask too many questions. I have taught many times over the lives I have lived, and the role of bumbling professor suits me well.

In this life I plan to write, put down my thoughts on what it is to be like me, immortal, a man for whom the sands of time do not touch. I hope also, to find more like me. There have been a few down the years who I have come into contact with, but there must be more. To understand this condition, the inability to age, to wither and die like everything else on this planet. To understand has been my driving force since the very beginning. I need to find others.

Chapter Two

BAPTISM OF LIFE

From what I am led to believe, and certainly what modern day historians have conjured up, I was born circa 1270. The second son of three, my father named me William. Tradition dictated a father name his first born son after himself, and keeping to such traditions the name William has followed me throughout my life.

In the year 1295 I was thrown in a Warders Prison, an outlaw and a murderer where, after several months of being fed just crumbs of bread and rotting Herring, I slowly starved and, again as the history books say, fell into a coma. I'm sure these days some of my memories of this time in my life are false memories, made up from what I have read, but one such memory I do know to be very real is my awakening from the dead.

News of my death had travelled fast and then news of my subsequent return from the grave caused the soothsayer Thomas the Rhymer to declare:

For sooth, ere he decease,
  Shall many thousands in the field make end.
  From Scotland he shall forth the Southron send,
  And Scotland thrice he shall bring to peace.
  So good of hand again shall ne'er be kenned.

Whether or not the man actually did speak these words is irrelevant really. News of my great awakening led storytellers to begin their embellishments until my name became legend, and I suppose this new found celebrity, in a time when there was no concept of fame, went to my head a little. I had stared death in the face and won, and now fearless, I knew where my destiny lay.

My legend grew, and with it support from my countrymen. We were to fight the oppression our country found itself under, and it was I, the second son of a mediocre Scottish landowner, who would lead the way. It wasn't until the battle of Stirling Bridge though when I found any wounds inflicted upon me would heal instantly.

My name now is unimportant, as I will be publishing this memoir either anonymously or simply by the pseudonym William, my name back then was Wallace and this is my story.

Others who pen their memoirs do so when their lives are coming to a close to try and find some sense to this crazy journey called life, but as I don't appear to suffer from the same affliction as those authors who have gone before me, I think that now I have waited for long enough. Still I search for others like me and I hope these pages reach them well.

It can be a lonely road to infinity if walked alone. This is my story, the story of my immortality, this is my journey. This is the memoir of my searching the world, searching faith, searching science, searching my own soul to find an answer to the questions I have asked since the Renaissance.

In putting pen to paper I am not sure where to start. People would implore me, and quite rightly so, to start at the beginning of this tale of my life, but the beginning is reasonably well documented already and I have no desire to rubbish historian's work by telling the tale of Wallace from 'the horse's mouth'. I know how difficult it is to search for people when there is little information available.

Instead I think I will begin this journey from Sterling Bridge, the battle in which we slaughtered our adversaries.

It was the morning of the 11th September 1297 when the English Army, heading north, found themselves bottlenecked having to cross Stirling bridge. Able to cross at a width of just two horsemen side by side, the English slowed to a halt as they crossed, their formations on the south side of the river Forth dispersed, and confusion ensued.

I lay in wait with my men on the north side of the bridge. When we estimated about two thousand troops had crossed we attacked. Unable to retreat and unable to push forward to allow more troops across to fight, the Scots sliced through those trapped on the north side. Some fled, swimming back across to the south of the river, but after the third push forward by infantry men and cavalry they realised the advantage was ours and the English retreated.

The biggest killer in battle is tiredness and fatigue, your senses dull, your body searches for more oxygen to power you limbs and this is when you become light headed and begin to slow. Soon after, your enemy has taken steel to your belly and you lie dying on the grass.

The years since I had woken from apparent near death had been kind to me physically. I found I was able to run great distances without tiring, my strength was unmatched, and as we attacked the remaining English infantry these attributes gave me great advantage. Despite my athleticism though, I met with the steel of a cornered Welsh infantryman. The searing white hot spike coursing through my middle sent me to the ground where I felt every breath I took sting every nerve ending.

As a twentieth century doctor I can diagnose that the sword pierced through my lower intestine, back through into my stomach and sliced through my left lung, severing my spinal cord. Back then all I saw was the pain and the icy fingers of the Grim Reaper incy-wincy spidering his way into my life to take it for his pleasure.

The Welsh solider followed me down to the ground, yanking for his sword so he could at least attempt to protect himself from the onslaught. As he pulled his weapon from my body the pain caused me to cry out, but before the cry had disappeared in the air I could feel pain no more.

Looking down at my stomach I indeed saw the

blood, but beyond that there was no wound from where it had come.

11 September 1297, Stirling Bridge, was when I discovered any wound inflicted upon me would heal. There would be many other battles in which I cheated death but Stirling was the first.

Chapter Three

POKERFACE

'Please, call me William,' I tell the Head of Medicine, the man who is, for all intents and purposes, my boss.

'As you wish William. I trust you're settled into your residence?'

I smile, nodding thanks to Professor Douglas as he sweeps his arm in the direction of the solitary chair in front of his desk. 'Yes the cottage is very comfortable and it saves me looking for accommodation.'

Douglas smiles, 'I'm afraid the previous occupant of the cottage left it in a bit of a mess, I trust you won't have any problems clearing any unwanted possessions out?'

I smile. 'I've spent all morning clearing up. Other than a few dying plants, the place is adequate.'

Leaning forward in his chair and tapping my letter of recommendation from Harvard which is laid out in front of him on his desk, Douglas says, 'Good. Now, Dr Dawson speaks very highly of you in this letter. I wonder, why is it you chose to leave such a prestigious posting, at Harvard no less, to come and teach here?'

'Well sir, in truth I wanted to come back to England. I spent many wonderful years over in America but for me it was time to come back home.'

'Hmmm,' he murmurs, tapping the letter once more.

Dr Dawson, the man who authored my letter, had just three years left at Harvard before he was due to retire, and his wife had lavish plans for when he finally put down his chalk and board duster. They were going to travel the world, perhaps buy a little place in Italy, dine out, live the life she had been waiting to live all these years, while unbeknown to her, Philip had spent those years squandering their retirement fund over the poker table. He fancied himself a gambler, and he was, just not a very good one.

I came across Philip Dawson two years ago as I was passing through Boston. I've played poker since its infancy, and to this day I'll state there is no better feeling than winning a big pot. Play the game for long enough though and you can spot the weak players a mile off, they reek of desperation. And that is exactly what poor Dr Dawson stunk of as I watched him lose his money over the felt.

Poker is a game of both skill and chance and you must respect both in equal measures. Players like our good Doctor believed his turn would come to be dealt the best hand, and indeed it always does, that is the element of chance, but it is the skill of the other players around the table which threw him off his winning hand every time.

For three nights I watched with interest at the bar of the late night underground gambling club. Then on the fourth night I sat down at the table and played with the Philip. Players love to chat and it soon became evident our loser was a Harvard Professor. That night I let him take my money. The next night I let him win a little more. The more he won from me the friendlier we became. On the third night I took him for everything he had, cash, expensive wrist watch his wife had bought him for their 30th wedding anniversary, and even the keys to his car parked a block away. He had been so smug sitting down at the table that evening, thought himself king of the world. By the end of the night he was a broken man, sobbing into his whiskey at the bar.

He explained his wife knew nothing of his gambling habit and with what he had won from me the previous few nights it had meant they could still afford to take that trip to the west coast they had planned for the following week. Now he didn't even have his car for the road trip.

I offered to bankroll his next game the following evening, perhaps he might win it all back then. And like a fool he agreed. The following night I joined him again for a whiskey after the game and this time I knew I had broken him. A fool and his money are easily parted, but a fool and someone else's money… lets just say he was happy to write any letter of recommendation for anyone if it meant me forgetting the debt and returning him his watch and car keys, and the rest of the money I had taken from him playing cards.

When the University had called Dr. Dawson to do the usual checks I believe the good professor could not have been more courteous about his former acquaintance, and was genuinely sorry to see me leave.

Now, you may think me heartless crushing a man, breaking him so that I might acquire leverage to use for my own gain, but I didn't force him to sit down at that table and play me. When you've played poker with men with pistols strapped to their belts in the late nineteen hundreds, you learn to either play well or pay well, I chose the former.

Professor Douglas stands up from behind his desk and holds out his hand, 'Well there appears to be nothing more to say other than welcome to The University of London. You can pick up your class roster from my secretary. I might sneak into a few of your first classes to see how you are bearing up.'

'I'll look forward to seeing you in there,' I tell him, shaking his hand and then leaving.

Once back at my new cottage I pour myself a large whiskey and pick up the telephone, ringing Chesterfield manor while looking around the small seating area. A potted plant by the door stands withering away. I must remember to throw it out, or perhaps I will attempt to save the wilted vegetation. It could be a pet project, reanimating that which is so close to its end.

'Hello?' Young Alan answers.

'Now what would you be doing sneaking around your uncle Eric's study, Al?'

Alan laughs, 'Uncle William hello. How is London?'

'The same as always only busier. How's Chesterfield Manor?'

'The same as always, only now Crazy Bill has been promoted from labourer to Farm Charge…'

'Alan,' I say in a stern tone, 'I've told you about calling him that. Have you actually sat down and spoken to the man?'

'Yes I have and he's nice. I believe he isn't drinking any longer, and he isn't really as strange, or as crazy, as I first thought. He and Uncle Eric are building a new pen for the sheep on the North-western field.'

'That's great. Is Eric around?'

'Uncle Ericccccc?' Al shouts through the house. A moment later I hear him approaching, scolding Alan for shouting so loud when he was only in the next room.

'It's Uncle William.'

'Hello? Doc?'

Since our first encounter he has always called me Doc, homage from the first time we met.

'And hello to you. How are you feeling?'

'A little restless, but that will pass. I've been keeping busy, keeping my mind active, this usually keeps the hunger at bay.'

Eric, despite his magnificence, has an insatiable yearning for blood. This craving has followed him through all of his lives, but together we are battling the monster which lives within him.

'How are you? How's London? You know the last

time I was there we met with Mr. Churchill, do you recall?'

Of course I do. With an infallible exterior also comes perfect memory retention. I remember it like it was this morning.

'I do. I also recall you and Winston getting into an argument.'

Eric laughs, 'You do like to keep some unusual friends Doc. How old was he when you saved his life?'

'Old enough to know better than to get captured by the Boers during that particular conflict.'

'Amen to that brother.'

A silence ensues. These small silences happen often between us, men who have seen so much in our lives and have grown tired of idle chit-chat. They are always companionable silences. We have spent enough years as friends to not have to fill the space with gossip and talk of the weather.

'So how's the weather?' I ask him.

Eric laughs, 'Piss off Doc.' Then hangs up.

I sit back smiling and take a sip of my whiskey. The day the weather becomes a talking point is the day I feel our friendship will have run its course.

Chapter Four

AFTERLIFE

On 23 August 1305 William Wallace was executed.

Hung, drawn, and quartered in front of a baying crowd at Smithfields, London. I watched amongst the spectators as my friend gave up his life so that I might rise again in another time. Big Duncan was the first person I entrusted my secret to and he went to the grave a hero in my eyes, taking my place under the executioner's falling axe. I think I owe my life to Duncan because as miraculous as some of the things I have both seen and experienced are, I do not believe I would survive a beheading.

That day I walked away from Smithfields and it

would be three hundred and two years before I returned to the island which housed two warring countries. With a little gold to aid my travels I set forth to France. This was a country I had known reasonably well as Wallace, but now I was a ghost. I did not have any identification to speak of, no papers signed by a higher master guaranteeing my good character and trustworthiness so that I might procure work. I was a nobody.

Fortunately I was reasonably educated and I could speak a few languages which would help as I hopped from country to country. With no real plan I bought passage on a night fishing boat from Dover to Calais, a crossing I still travel to this day, and landed in France the following morning.

The idea was simple, to find more of my kind. Even back then I knew it could not just be me, destined to walk the planet alone, the immortal nomad.

Was I an angel?

Was I a God?

These were times before my faith in the almighty had fallen to the might of reason. Mr Darwin would not write his own book for another five hundred years and the Christian God was all I had ever known.

I prayed to that God each night, asking for guidance, a sign to show me the way, a light in the darkest of skies. I spent my days traveling south and my nights drinking in whichever local inn was available, listening for stories of the unusual, of any lead which might bring me closer to meeting another like me.

I would experiment on myself, take a blade to my flesh and watch as the skin sealed itself back up. I would leap from great cliff faces, the closest I would ever feel to flying, and when at the bottom of the ravine, my body bloody and broken, I would marvel at how it would repair itself. The blinded eye's vision would become crystal clear once more, the snapping and crunching of bones resetting themselves as I writhed on the ground in agony.

There had to be a reason for this. Man did not repair themselves like this, and I needed to find out why I was able to. Alone in the world, and with no one to confide in about my gift, I decided to reinvent myself. This would be the first of many incarnations. I cut my hair, sheared off the famous Wallace beard, and headed through Spain, down to Morocco, seeking out the wisest of men in each town I travelled through and asking these men of any rumoured witches or sorcerers. To be able to meet with those who possessed the powers of magic could lead me in the right direction. I sought out many witch doctors and alchemists on my road east through North Africa and then crossed over to Italy, always wary of revealing my true intentions.

Once in Italy there was one man in whom I put my trust.

His name was Giovanni Correggio, a respected scholar and alchemist based at the University of Bologna. I met Giovanni in 1347 while reading the classics at Bologna, and we immediately became good friends. Despite my youthful appearance Giovanni often commented I had a wise man's mind and marvelled at how I was able to speak so fluently in so many languages despite claiming I hadn't ever left Italy. In truth I was now in my seventh decade on this planet and were it not for my youthful exterior, would be considered very old.

I was interested in Giovanni's mind, his ideas of a magical nature, but I knew it was my body Giovanni wanted, lusted over. Despite this he never propositioned me sexually and our relationship was always platonic as we talked of alchemy and myths and legends surrounding the magical science of the time.

Giovanni told me a tale that in 1329, some eighteen years previous, he had known a man who had drunk from the fountain of youth, a whimsical fellow who had travelled through Italy much as I had been doing before setting down camp to attend the University of Bologna.

We spoke at great length of the man who claimed that he did not age, that he had found the fountain of youth and bathed in its waters. The Traveller (this being the name he introduced himself as) said he had been around since before God himself. Laughed at, at first, and then chased out of town for blasphemy, Giovanni last saw The Traveller heading on the road to Rome, calling back that he would seek court with the King of Italy, Louis IV.

What became of that proposed meeting? Giovanni never found out. The traveller disappeared, never to be heard of again.

Eighteen years later and now I knew for certain there was another with my own penchant for living. This encouraged me to continue my search, and I would journey along the very road The Traveller had taken, a road plagued with death as there were rumours from the south the Black Death was travelling north with the rats.

'Please William, do not leave,' Giovanni pleaded when I told him of my plans, 'You have become the reason for an old man to keep breathing.'

I reached across to the man six years my junior and kissed him on the forehead, 'I must leave my friend. You have known for some time I am not like others, my ability to speak in many tongues, the stories I have shared with you…I must now continue upon my journey.'

'But my dear William, why would you leave me here, a rotting corpse like the rest of them?'

There were no words. In the four years I had called Bologna my home Giovanni had become a trusted friend and I don't know why I decided to impart my secret to him as I was leaving, but I did.

'My friend,' I told him as we sat at his kitchen table the night before I was due to leave. Giovanni had laid out a platter of breads and cheeses, olive oil, and wine to wash the late evening meal down with. I picked up a sharp knife used for slicing the cheese and twirled it through my fingers. 'You know I will be saddened to leave tomorrow morning, to wave farewell to you after these many years we have been friends.'

Giovanni smiled at this and I reached across to take his hand in mine, showing him my naked palm and the underside of my wrist.

'You know William, that I love you so…'

I nodded and replied quickly, 'Yes I know.'

Giovanni laughed, the tears rolling down his face, 'Look at me, an old man crying like a love sick woman.'

Squeezing his hand, I told him, 'And I too love you my friend. You have been a great companion these past years but I feel I have not been entirely truthful with you.'

'Oh?'

'I too am an old man, and I only tell you this now because tomorrow, when I leave I fear I will not return for many years and by then you will be gone.'

Giovanni stood up, frowning as he paced back and forth in the small kitchen, 'William why do you talk like this?'

'Because I seek the truth, and I think one truth may follow another. Watch.'

I slid the knife's blade down the middle of my forearm, watching as blood seeped from beneath the steel.

'Oh no, why do you do this,' Giovanni cried out, rummaging along his food preparation area for a towel or cloth.

'Gio stop,' I shouted and the old man froze, slowly turning back to face me. He looked into my eyes and I smiled, 'Look at my arm.'

He shook his head, tears streaming down his face, 'I'm sorry William but no. I fear for what you want to show me, fear the two possible outcomes to your actions, that if you bleed out you will die and I will lose you forever, and if you do not then everything I have ever known means nothing.'

With our eyes locked, Giovanni refusing to watch

my arm heal, I nodded, 'I'm sorry, but I suppose now you can at least take comfort in knowing why I must leave, to search for more like me.'

He shook his head, 'Oh my dear William, but I figured it out long ago. My only regret now is telling you about The Traveller. If I had not mentioned him then you would have perhaps stayed for a few more years, given this old man the pleasure of your company until it was time for me to depart this world.'

Turning away he then asked me to leave, and that was the last time I saw my friend, the first person to whom I entrusted my secret.

Chapter Five

CRAZY BILL

In 1910 I took a position at the University of Cambridge teaching the next generation Biology and Anatomy, but it would turn out my post imparting knowledge on that particular generation would be cut short due to the outbreak of the Great War and Britain joining the battle on 4th August 1914. The majority of my students left to fight for their country on the Western Front.

I had opted to stay out of this particular war.

Over the centuries I have had my fill of bloodshed, and I was exempt from being forced to fight in this new war, but as more and more of my students headed off to Europe I realised this war would present me with an opportunity.

We had all heard the stories which filtered back from The Front, of whole platoons being wiped out by the enemy during a charge through No Man's Land. This was indeed an opportunity for someone forever seeking others who do not fall. Like me at Stirling Bridge, there could be many a man who would wake from their annihilation whole again, and now with a new weapon in their arsenal, the need not to fear death ever again.

Looking up at my students, I smile, 'And that concludes today's lecture introducing you to the human anatomy. I'm sure you young men learn more about this particular subject with your girlfriends…or someone else's girlfriend, on a Friday night after a belly full of ale and an array of promises you have no intention of keeping. Am I preaching to those already more knowledgable than I, I wonder?'

A rumbling of nervous laughter and a few red faces finishes my first lecture of the term and it is good to be back, imparting my knowledge, passing it on to the next generation who will soon rule the world.

As the students clear out, I notice Professor Douglas sat at the back of the classroom.

'Sir,' I say, nodding as he makes his way down to the front.

'A most enlightened and energetic lecture,' he tells me. 'I especially enjoyed your closing comments, and so too did the students. That's good, it builds rapport with them. You will be seen by them as relatable, approachable.'

I shrug, gathering up my papers, 'I've found injecting a little humour into the class does wonders for a student's motivation.'

Douglas nods, 'I recall falling asleep in many of my lectures as a boy, my word they were dull, presented by a mono-toned Professor named Dearden.'

'We have a lot of information to impart. I've found a little entertainment never does any harm.'

'Hmm, quite so…' he says, pausing.

I turn to him and smile, 'Was there anything else sir?'

'Yes, during your lecture I was wondering if you might be the perfect temporary replacement for Professor Waybridge, who has taken ill.'

'You'd like me to take over his history lectures?' I ask.

'My, my William, you *are* well informed.'

'I have a good memory.'

'That you do. Not once did I see you consulting your papers while delivering your lecture. Were they placed on the table just for show?'

We both laugh, and I say, 'It would appear a little strange to the class if I didn't have props.'

History.

If ever there is a subject matter I am more than qualified to teach it is this.

'Dr Dawson's letter of recommendation stated you were a History Professor at Harvard as well as teaching Medicine. I do wonder how a man as young as you has managed to fit it all in?'

Time my friend. Plenty of it.

'I'm at your disposal, sir,' I tell Douglas.

'Excellent. Then perhaps you might like to join me and some of the other teachers for our weekly get-together tonight at my house? It'll give me a chance to introduce you to everyone.'

'I'll be there,' I say, and he nods his approval, writing down his address and underlining 7pm twice.

History, something created automatically through the passing of time. We all have it, our own histories. There is no escaping it as it has already happened. My history spans centuries but is no more remarkable than a new born child's. It acts as marker points through ones life, through the life of the planet and the universe, and once a moment in time passes from the present into the past it becomes history. Enough time passes and history is forgotten, but this is not to say that moment was any less relevant than this, just as no one grain of sand is more important than the last when falling through the eye of an hourglass.

The history of reinventions for me has been a varied affair. My first few identities were created by forgers, but others I would kill for, taking up a lonely traveller's mantle and continuing on my own travels as this person. Back then my reinventions were a simple affair. I would say farewell to the people I had lived my "life" around and be on my way, following the horizon in search of the ever elusive immortal. If I returned to a town I had called home, I would only do so after enough time had passed so that even the town's young children upon my previous departure would have since passed, old men and women having succumbed to their ageing, unable to beat their falling grains of sand.

Further through the years, as the world opened up and people travelled more widely, there was need for documents to prove I was who I said I was. For this I would seek out master forgers to invent my new lives for me. These documents always came with a hefty price tag though, but one I would always pay for.

With the centralisation of governments and travel becoming more accessible to all, the need for passports became commonplace. Instead of visiting forgers for these documents, I sought out people happy to trade their own identities for generous compensations.

The common man does not travel the world, even now as the 1950s come to a close. The common man works to provide for his family and stays within their town or city for most of their life. They lay roots, have children, watch those children grow, staying close when their offspring go forth and multiply. The common man would happily trade his birth certificate and buy a passport, paid for by me. Giving something up which has no value to them in return for a mighty windfall, is no hardship for them.

On this particular occasion I was lucky finding such a man who was also called William. Whenever possible I have always tried to keep my birth name as it acts as a reminder of who I am, my own roots which keep me grounded and are a reminder of my lifelong quest, to find others who are like me, immortal.

This was also the reason I had spent the past six months with Eric and Alan at Chesterfield Manor. It takes time acquiring genuine identity documents which will become the foundation of my new life. A forger would have a new life on paper for me inside of two weeks, but when you want the real thing you first must find a willing participant.

William, I found on a trip into town one afternoon with Alan. The man was sat on a local park bench drinking whiskey straight out of the bottle.

'Stay away from him Uncle William,' Alan told me, 'That's crazy Bill. He came back from the war strange, like father.'

Looking at "crazy" Bill as we passed, I assumed he must have been young still when the second war ended.

The next day I returned to the park alone and sat down next to Mr. Crazy. It didn't take long for us to start talking. We talked for an hour about the war and I asked Bill what it was he wanted from this life now the war had been over for some thirteen years, what were his dreams.

'A job, a sense of purpose, a warm bed to fall asleep in every night, maybe someday a woman who would love me and let me love her back…'

I smiled. Isn't that all anyone really dreams of in this life?

'What if I was to help you get these things? Not the love of a good woman, I'm afraid you would have to find that yourself, but what if I was able to set you on the right path? Would you take the opportunity?'

Our friend William began to sob. Great big sorrowful tears ran down his cheeks, and he turned to me, nodding.

'Do you know Chesterfield Manor?' I asked.

'Of course. The big house on the hill.'

'I believe their farm is looking for labourers. I am friends with the owner, perhaps I might put in a good word for you?'

"Crazy" Bill shook his head, 'Sorry sir, but I have nowhere to live…'

'What if I bought a house for you to live in? There is a small cottage for sale just over the green. Could you see yourself living in a place overlooking this wonderful park?'

More tears, and then, 'But why would you help me? What is it you have to gain?'

I smiled once more, 'We'll come to that. First though, let's see about getting you that warm bed you speak so fondly of.'

I bought the house for William to live in, I got him the job at Chesterfield Farm, and I helped him open up an account with the local bank, depositing £200 into it so he might buy some new clothes and furniture for his new house.

Within a week "Crazy" Bill was working hard at Chesterfield farm. The farm's manager told me he had never seen a grafter like him. Within a month, clean shaven and wearing new clothes, and with a confidence about him from getting his life on track, he caught the eye of a local woman.

All of Bill's dreams had come into fruition and when I joined him one evening at his place it was time for me to make my move.

'You know William, it is nice to see you smile. Could it be love?'

He flushed, turning his reddened face from me for a moment before saying, 'She is one of a kind. I have never felt so happy to be alive. Thank you for everything. When we met I was nearing the end, a lost soul. I never imagined a future for myself and now I do.'

'That's good to hear. Now tell me, this house…'

'Which I have always insisted paying you rent for…' Bill added quickly.

I laughed, clapping the man on the shoulder, 'How would you like to own it?'

'What?'

'It would come at a price, but one I feel you could afford.'

There was no pause to consider my offer, he shook my hand as soon as I held it out for him.

The next day we sent off for his passport, with my photograph attached of course, and Bill traded me his birth certificate for the cottage.

When the passport office rang to arrange an interview due to "me" being off the grid since the war, I was already in possession of a new drivers licence and I took along the newly acquired deeds to the house with me. It was all the identification I needed to be issued with the means to travel the world as William.

A month or so later the passport arrived and I bid farewell to a man who had become my friend over the passing months. I told him I would keep in contact, and if ever he needed anything or got into trouble, he could contact me.

I admit this endeavour has meant putting faith in this man, but I believe he won't betray me. He spent too many years out in the cold. As far as he is concerned I gave him his life back. He doesn't understand that by giving me his birth certificate and sending off for the passport he has returned the favour and given me his life also. A life I am now settling into as a teacher at the University of London.

Chapter Six

BATTLESCARS

I have loved many women in my time, taken many wives, and given life to many sons and daughters. I do not feel my prolonged life has been a curse, indeed for almost two hundred years I have been on a quest to try and understand why it is my cells regenerate at such an alarming rate, and why only the very few have been granted such gifts.

I remember the first time I was shot, within minutes I was up and about as though nothing had happened. If it had been anyone else witnessing my radical recovery I believe things may not have turned out quite the same for me, but as it was, it was my Corporal who watched in amazement as my organs repaired themselves and then my chest cavity closed.

The year was 1916 and I had joined the 1st battalion of the York & Lancaster regiment two months into their campaign on the Somme. Having seen so much bloodshed already in my life when the Great War (the war to end all wars) broke out I was happy staying out of this one. At the time I was passing myself off as a forty year old Professor of English at Cambridge University and was exempt from fighting in the war. It was only when I started to see more and more young men leaving the town to go and fight that I too signed up. I couldn't sit back and watch the mortal give their lives while I knew I could perhaps make a difference.

After passing basic fitness training we were shipped off to the Somme where I was awarded the rank of Captain. It was only a few days later while enjoying a quiet cigarette on night watch when I was introduced to Corporal Chesterfield.

'Captain sir,' said a voice in the dark. I turned and saw no one, but then into the moonlight moved Eric. 'I have been posted onto night watch with you sir.'

I smiled. It had been over a century and a half since I had saved Richard Woodley from his villagers questioning his mortality. At first I believe he may not have recognised me, if he did he certainly did not show it.

The first night on watch together was uneventful and we scarcely spoke. In the trenches there is much silence and contemplation, we are alone in this world and we hope to get back home to see our families.

'Who are you back home sir?' Eric asked me on the second night of our posting together.

'I am a professor at Cambridge University, and you?'

My words hung on the cool night air for a very long time. Eventually he answered, his voice hoarse like the cries of the wounded we could hear further down the line, the day's casualties from no man's land.

'I am a student back home, studying to join the priesthood.'

'A very noble profession my good man, but why then might I ask, do you find yourself on the Western Front? Surely you might find yourself exempt from enlisting if your path was for something greater?'

Eric then took his time to turn and face me before saying, quite clearly, 'The very same reason you find yourself watching over the tides of death night after night.'

I nodded at this. I had been wrong, the man had recognised me from his grandson's funeral and I would not shame myself to try and deny that Dr Steel had not been yet another alias of mine. Instead I stood up from my perch and held out my hand. Eric grasped it with a firm grip and stood to meet my gaze.

'Why did you intervene that day three life times ago? How did you know?'

I shrugged my shoulders and told him, 'I have spent almost my entire life searching for men like myself, the divine who possess a further step in the evolutionary chain.'

Eric shook his head, 'Let me stop you right there because if not we will be a loggerheads with one another all night. I am a follower of the Lord, I respect your opinion but let us not discuss the point of origin of our gifts because you will think me naive just as I will see you as a blasphemer.'

Although I wanted him to listen, although I felt I needed to sit him down and talk to him about natural selection, explain how the myth of a God was in fact instilled upon civilisations long before either of us were born, as a form of control, and that the first worshipping civilisations in fact worshipped the earth, making them naturists and, in a sense, non-believers also, I felt to follow this course might alienate my new found comrade.

Instead I simply nodded and said, 'Understood,'

and we spoke at length of our experiences. While I imagined us the same when I came by the quiet Mr Woodley living in the rural Lancashire dales, throughout our discussions I found subtle differences in our evolutions which made me question my theories of how the divine came to live amongst man.

Back then I had yet to discover the likes of rapid cell regeneration, and DNA mapping was light years away, but I imagined us as the next step. For the fittest to survive they had to adapt themselves to the ever changing world, and the most perfect form of survival would be to regenerate tissue mass quicker than it might diminish. In Eric I became aware of more startling feats of divinity, but first it seemed I would show my hand.

The day I was shot was the day almost our whole platoon was wiped out. We were ordered over the top and into no man's land to make a push for the German lines. Upon our briefing we were led to believe the enemy had all but vacated the trenches we were soon hoping to call our own. Throughout the morning, heavy artillery bombarded our destination with the most awesome fire power no mortal man could ever hope to survive, and with Corporal Chesterfield by my side we led the attack. No sooner had we made it out of our trenches we were annihilated with heavy machine gun fire, mortars, and the crack aim of German sharp shooters. Further forward we pushed, zigzagging across the barren landscape, through swampy foxholes and the cries of our dying comrades. And then I felt the wind being taken out of me not twenty yards from the enemy line, but still further I pushed forward, deafened by the constant stream of fire, blinded by mud kicked up from the ground, unaware all this time I was in fact the last man still upright and still pushing forward. Another shot, this time catching me in the arm and I was spun around with the sheer force. As I fell to my knees, my back now to the enemy, I surveyed the ground I had crossed, now littered with the debris of the men who had followed me to their deaths. I was completely alone, and then, seemingly to appear from out of thin air Eric picked me up and lunged us both into a watery foxhole.

'My God you're hit,' he cried out, his arm around my neck to keep my head from falling under the murky swamp, maroon with the blood of men lost underneath our feet.

I laughed at this comment for some reason. Maybe it was the shock and adrenaline battling through my system, I don't know, but when I peered down at my torso I watched with Eric as my fatal wounds healed. A few moments later I was as fit and as healthy as the day

William Wallace was hung drawn and quartered for the baying crowd at Smithfield in London.

'Are you ready for that final push sir?' Eric shouted into my ringing ears as I knelt forward, heaving at the stench of the rotting bodies which shared our hole.

Later Eric told me I had grinned wildly at this suggestion and charged with a feral like fury spurring me on. As we reached the enemy's line Eric appeared to jump the barbed webbing which was there to keep us out, landing upon two German soldiers and as he gutted one with his bayonet he sunk his teeth into the neck of the second, ripping out his jugular and then gutting this man also.

It was a massacre. Two invincible English knights against the frightened army of the Hun. We were both awarded medals for our courageous valour, but unfortunately upon our next skirmish in no man's land we did not return to be able to collect them. Neither of our bodies were recovered and given a proper Army burial, but hey, that's life.

I had found a contemporary with whom I shared a bond which most of humanity would not understand. We were the same but different, and as the Great War ended Eric and I travelled across the Atlantic to America. In order to understand our gifts we would need to employ only the brightest teams of scientists to help us figure out what exactly our gifts were and how they worked. This would need money, and in 1920 Prohibition in the United States enabled us to earn more money than we would ever need. It was also in the year 1920 that I found out to what extent Eric's gifts had hold over him.

I often enjoy finding myself transported back to a much simpler time, when the grey areas in society were few. Man knew right from wrong, man policed his own life, and if man was wronged then he would seek to put that wrong-doing right. Things change, friends, family, and loved ones die, and I move on. It seems it is just Eric and I who are destined to walk hand in hand upon this earth for all of eternity. I have found few others with the ability to live beyond their years and this worries me somewhat. It means, for one, that Darwin was inaccurate in his theory of evolution. Maybe I still have a long search ahead, or maybe I am not looking hard enough. I know there are people out there who can do some amazing things, and I wish they would help me help us all to understand our purpose on this earth. Darwin's theory of evolution through natural selection states the purpose of life is to reproduce, to pass on life so that future generations can do the same, and slowly throughout time all species will either adapt to their ever changing world, or die out. If this is true then why have I watched my sons and daughters live and die so many times over?

With all of them long dead and buried I am beginning to feel like maybe time is running out for me. There are people in this world who know about me, although only one or two a century has always been my rule. When too many discover the impossible they begin to wonder if there is any personal gain in this knowledge. I have, in the past, trusted too many men at once with my secret so that they could help me discover more like me quickly, for their lives are short. This has always ended in disaster and resulted in me having to disappear, assume a new identity, and often slay the betrayers. Despite this my search must continue. It is what drives my very existence. To figure out the big why am I here is all that really matters in the end.

Chapter Seven
================

AN OLD FRIEND

I tend to enjoy these little get-togethers. I have been the "new one" at so many schools through the years, these introductions are second nature to me. I have also on many occasions been in Professor Douglas's position, introducing the new blood to all the weathered veterans.

'Phylis, Geoff, I'd like to introduce you both to William.'

They both smile, shaking my hand. Geoff is an English Professor and Phylis his wife.

'The man who teaches everything,' Geoff smiles.

'Now now, leave the man alone. Derek Waybridge

deciding he is ill again put great strain on our already understaffed faculty. William here has come to the rescue and my headaches in the evening are less intense because of it.'

We all laugh and I say, 'It a pleasure. I am, at heart, a historian.'

'A historian, a Doctor, are there any other attributes we might pair you with?' Phylis asks.

'I can play the piano. Learned years ago and I find losing myself in music most soothing.'

'Do you compose?' Professor Douglas asks me.

'No,' I laugh, 'I only play what men greater than myself have composed.'

'A man with many talents,' Geoff remarks and I nod politely as Douglas leads me off towards a huddle of students in the corner.

'Gentlemen, may I introduce to you our new Professor.'

The three young men nod, eager to shake my hand and they each introduce themselves.

'Smith sir.'

'Clay.'

And as the last young man holds out his hand I pause. Even in this day and age where people are able to travel the world and find a life for themselves on the other side of the planet, it is unusual to meet a man from the Far East in England, especially one so young.

'Chester, sir. Apie Chester,' the boy says, shaking my hand.

'Which is a contradiction in terms sir as he's never blimming 'appy,' Smith or Clay says, and they all laugh.

'Now, now, gentlemen, that's no way to talk about our oriental friend,' Douglas says.

'Whereabouts are you from?' I ask the man.

'Thailand. But my great grandfather was from here, well, not London, he came from the north.'

'Ah, a fellow northerner by family, William. Excellent.'

'Indeed,' I say, keeping in mind I am frowning at this young man. There is reason for that. I know this man. He is a little older than when I last saw him, but it is he.

'Tell me Apie, what are you studying here at this great University?' I ask.

'History, sir.'

That figures.

'Like you William, Mr Chester has just started his first year here with us,' Douglas says.

I smile, holding out my hand for him again, 'Well it would appear we will be seeing more of each other Apie…' I say, accentuating his name.

As our eyes lock for a moment I know without a doubt it is him, The Chinaman. This was a name the other soldiers gave him in the trenches on the Western Front, but to me he was called Apinya, and that great grandfather he spoke of is Peter Chesterfield, Alan's big brother, Eric's nephew, and a man who, at this moment in 1958, is just thirty four years old, a little young to be a great grandfather you might say, but this particular great grandson is not from here, this time. Apinya Chesterfield will not be born for another fifty one years.

Douglas takes my arm and leads me off to be introduced to some more teachers, and when I glance back I see Apinya, sorry, "Apie" is watching me leave. He smiles and winks at me.

I'm guided through the rest of the evening with more introductions, answering the same questions over and over. Yes I will be teaching both Medicine *and* History, no I don't know how I've managed to fit it all in either, what with being so young still and all. The wine flows, the back patting and self congratulation continues, and all the time I keep an eye on my future History student. Back when we met in the trenches he was so pleased to see me, but now I'm not so sure.

As the evening draws to a close, I hang back, taking

my time to finish the last of the wine. Apie Chester is still chatting to his friend Smith or Clay, the third one of them leaving earlier after he fell asleep drunk in the water closet.

'So my boy,' a rather intoxicated Professor Douglas says, slapping me on the back, 'How do you feel now you've met everybody?'

'Eager to get to work. You have a great faculty here sir,' I tell him.

As Apie shakes his friend's hand and approaches us, I step back.

'Thank you for inviting me this evening Professor Douglas, it has been a wonderful night.'

'My pleasure Mr. Chester. I trust you introduced yourself to a few other professors? It really is a shame Professor Waybridge could not attend. With your fascination for history he really is the man to talk to, although I'm sure William here will make an admirable temporary replacement.'

I smile, nodding and Apinya turns to me. 'Actually, sir, I was wondering if I might talk to you about the upcoming year?'

Douglas laughs, 'It's always work, work, work with you young men.'

Apinya flushes and shrugs.

'Certainly,' I say, shaking Professor Douglas's hand

and wishing him a pleasant evening and then leaving with Mr. Chester.

As we step out onto the pavement, I turn to the boy and he smiles, 'It's good to see you William. How long has it been for you?'

'Forty-Two years, you?'

Apinya grins, 'Three.'

We then look each other up and down and burst out laughing, hugging one another like the old friends we are.

'You're looking well. Tell me, have you seen Eric?' I ask.

'No. I may travel up there in a few days but the reason I'm here right now is to see you.'

'And you enrolled in University just to get close? How did you even find me?'

Apinya smirks, nodding his head towards me. Me. Of course. The boy who knows the future has experienced times in my long life which have yet to come still for me. There was a time when I imagined my kind were the most remarkable beings in this world. That was until I met young Apinya in the trenches in 1916 a few weeks before meeting Eric for the first time. Eric, I had recognised from a previous life, but Apinya, Apinya recognised me from a life I had yet to live.

We talk as we walk slowly back towards my cottage.

I ask him about his life in the next century and he nods, telling me of an organisation he has become involved with where more and more people like myself have come forward. He talks of terrorist attacks, viruses plaguing the world, and, more fondly, he talks about Chesterfield Manor and a lady in his life.

'So you are in love?' I ask.

'Ever since I was nine years old.'

'And Eric, are you still close to him?'

Apinya smiles, 'More than you could understand right now.'

I too smile. When we first met in the war, Apinya told me that he had known me since he was a little boy, that I was instrumental in him understanding and honing an ability he could not fathom and could not control. I'm happy to see this young man and I look forward to the first time he meets me, as a young boy far from home.

As we approach my door I turn and ask him if he'd like to join me for a nightcap.

Apinya declines, 'Next time perhaps. For now I would like to ask something of you.'

'Anything, old friend.'

'Start writing your memoirs. I know you have been thinking about it. I know you feel a little apprehensive about putting pen to paper. Just do it. The world I am from, it relies upon your book being published. Your words start a chain reaction which will mean hundreds of people will one day have a home, understand who they are.'

'Hundreds? You say there are hundreds?'

Apinya shakes my hand as I open my door, 'No, there are many more. Start writing William, and I'll see you in class.'

Chapter Eight

THE NOMAD

Once in Rome I was fortunate enough to procure the services of an artist. A man able to copy any form of identification, documents, transcripts, and for a few gold coins my artist created a life which I was ready to jump into.

I had come to the conclusion that in order to find more of my contemporaries I should first look inwards at myself, learn all there was to learn about the physicality of my own body. This drew me towards medical school where, in my first year, I was looked upon with suspicion. What was an outsider doing learning with men who appeared so much younger than him? If only they knew.

I kept a sense of humour with the occasional teasing from my classmates.

'I spent a lot of time travelling in my youth,' I would explain to my class mates, 'Not really sure what I would like to study.'

'So you decided medicine? I think perhaps you didn't travel far enough,' a class mate had replied and I agreed with him.

The science of medicine in Europe in the mid-fourteen hundreds was barbaric. I should have travelled further East. In Europe, medical knowledge passed down from former civilisations had been lost, but at the same time the Muslim world had managed to retain most of its medical knowledge and was far more advanced. In Europe, doctors were superstitious barbarians, believing in prayer when all was lost. Had I moved further East, I think my education would have benefitted.

The human anatomy was still largely unknown at the time and it appeared the only way in which I might learn more about our bodies was as a butcher-surgeon on the battlefield. There I would learn first-hand the endurance man's body was put through.

Having fifty years earlier been the cause of so many

injuries on the field of battle, the irony was not lost on me as I knelt down in the bloody mud amputating a fallen soldier's leg. Out there, in the aftermath of battle, is where I learned more about the human body and the spirit of the dying than any classroom could unveil. Text books and stuffy professors can only teach you so much.

Ten years later I was one of those stuffy professors myself. By day I'd teach students all that I had seen and learned amidst the dying, and at night I would trawl Rome's surrounding townships, aware that soon I would have to move on, that fifteen years in Italy had been too long, but I loved the country, the people, and even when the Black Death struck across Europe I couldn't think of anywhere else I'd rather be.

In 1363 I was offered a placement in Athens teaching medicine and the art of the barbarism we at the time called surgery, but by now I had begun to tire of God getting in the way of science. Patients were told to pray to their God and doctors would stand by, unwilling to do anything but continue practicing outdated techniques. Little, it seems, has changed in some ways even now in the middle of the twentieth century.

I knew it was too early, that technology hadn't progressed enough for my answers, and so I took off again in search of the Divine, not God, I'd had enough of Him having lived in Rome for a decade and a half. I wanted to find my brothers and sisters, the angels who walked the Earth. I wanted to find The Traveller.

I bid farewell to my students and set sail East, first through Greece, not to teach (I had taken my fill of imparting my knowledge for the time being). I revisited my Nomadic urges and travelled around, learning the languages and cultures first hand as I made my way through towns, countries and empires alike. I sat at the table of kings in the Ottoman Empire, bellied down around campfires along desert roads with simple goat herders in north Africa. I travelled and I learned their words, listened to their stories. When asked I would confess to once being a teacher, when pushed I would explain I had nothing more to teach, that it was time for me to fill up on new knowledge so that I may one day impart that wisdom upon children who knew no better.

I followed leads, spoke to wise men who were rumoured to be sorcerers, tracked down old ladies who were whispered to be witches, but none were like me so still I searched. I fought in wars I did not care for, and fought furiously on the battlefield, always keeping in mind others who fought as I did, but there were none who rose from the ground after meeting with the stroke of steel.

As the 1300s drew to a close I found myself alone in a world I was beginning to become detached from. I was bitter and Godless. I had spent too many years on both sides of the battlefield and had seen the death of so many men for what it was, a power struggle for the church, wanting to rule the world and stopping at nothing. My eyes were opened and I saw what religion really was, a means of controlling the masses.

Blood had followed me for over a century and I was still no closer to discovering why I was able to heal and had stopped ageing many years ago. Frustrated and with nowhere to turn, I decided to move north to the Netherlands. I landed in Amsterdam in 1403 looking for peace and setting myself up as the town Doctor's assistant, renting out the small flat above the practice.

Life slowed down for me.

I integrated myself into the town and became one of them. The pleasant foreigner from Italy soon discovered a different pace of life and that suited him fine. Always with my ear to the ground I listened for stories, myths, and legends of the unusual, but none came. Instead, for the first time I could remember in this life or my previous, I learned to relax and I stopped worrying about the Divine, the mysterious Traveller, and my ability. I began to live my life,

As horribly clichéd as it is nowadays, my boss Dokter Brusten's daughter became somewhat infatuated with the tall, often bumbling Italian (I was still getting to grips with the Dutch language) and she was there at every opportunity to help me settle in. Else Brusten was a plain looking young lady of nineteen. Slim with dark blonde hair, dark eyes, her face not unattractive but in no way what one might have deemed pretty for the day. Fiercely protective of her father and mother, she was an only child who sought to better herself by learning all her father had to teach. She had aspirations for herself which I admired, and then she fell in love with me and everything changed.

We married six months after me arriving in Holland and a year later we celebrated bringing our first child into the world. Hans was a delight, huge inquisitive eyes, always following his doting father around. When little Nessie was born two years on from Hans, I felt for the first time content. My life had been filled with something I had never known before now and my family brought me so much joy, but the years rearing my son and daughter flew by all too quickly.

My boy Hans had decided to follow in the footsteps of both his father and grandfather and left for medical school in Bruge in the summer of 1423. Little Nessie was already courting a local boy from a good, respectable family, and so it seemed soon the once noisy household Else and I had created would quieten some.

I had spent two good decades content in living my life as one should, creating and bringing up my children, but now I had begun to feel the community turning on me somewhat. My agelessness was beginning to show. In the fifteen hundreds one did not physically look as I did at the supposed age of fifty. Back then one was lucky to live this long in the first place.

At first it was simple comments, friends and colleagues saying how well I looked, all the while Else aged rapidly by my side. Else began to worry for herself and the children as town folk began to talk. I had never tried to keep my secret from my wife you see, she learned long ago of my 'magic', had even invited it in our own children, as had I. Slowly though, down the years, I watched as the creeping doubt had set in Else's eyes. Was I magic or was it a trick, was I the devil?

These were simple times and simple, God fearing people. Else knew I had never been one to speak in kind of the Lord and now she was beginning to cultivate her own ideas about the truth behind my ability.

Had old man Brusten still been alive I would have had an ally, someone to talk sense to my wife, his daughter, as Dokter Brusten had first and foremost been a man of science and not whimsical myth, but Brusten had died the previous decade.

The day I approached *him* with my secret was a day which changed both of our lives for the better, because in my boss and father-in-law I had found a contemporary with whom I could work with to try and answer some of the questions I had.

'Come, my son, sit down and show me again,' Dokter Brusten cried out with childlike enthusiasm each time we would meet outside of work hours to discuss my immortality.

We would sit ourselves down in his surgery and I would roll up my sleeves while he took out a knife. I would then show him and watch him watch me with wonder every time when my wound healed before our eyes.

'In your time in the Warders prison in Scotland, as you slowly starved to death, was there nothing you might remember that would appear odd?'

With Dokter Brusten's help we had pieced together when I had changed and became something more than mortal. At first we had argued it must have been at Stirling Bridge, when the Welsh solider had stabbed me but then thinking back there had never been an instant where I had not felt one hundred percent since my incarceration before the uprising back in Scotland.

'Papa no, I think about these times constantly but there is nothing. The cell was sparse, the food infrequent and dreadful. I fell into a deep sleep from which the doctor could not wake me and thought me dead. Perhaps I did die.'

'Perhaps.'

'And was then reborn?'

With a grin Dokter Brusten raised his hands and laughed, 'Anything is possible my son. What we must find out somehow is if you have passed your gifts down to your children.'

Before the town and a confused Else could turn on me, I left Amsterdam. Twenty two years after arriving I became a Nomad once more and with a tear in my eye for the family and the memories I would leave behind in this place, I headed back on the road though this journey called life.

Chapter Nine

WHAT HAPPENED ALWAYS HAPPENS

I pour myself a coffee and sit down at the small desk in the corner of the sitting room, searching for inspiration. The dying plant does nothing to tickle my muse and so I turn to face the wall. In front of me I have a leather-bound Journal, every page blank but I hope to remedy that. I've had word from the future that I must write the memoirs I have been considering for many years. The last time I tried revealing to the world our existence I was met with laughter. It was a trick. One you might see at a circus or magic show. I was merely a magician.

People close their minds to the impossible, look for a rational explanation, of which I have none.

In writing this memoir I would be able to reach far more people than I ever was able to while travelling from town to town. Also, because of the nature of the world we now live in, man has changed. When I was travelling around Europe, moving from town to town, following whispers of the impossible, man was a superstitious soul. These days they are cynical and the stories of people displaying feats of magnificence died with man's innocence.

And so I must start again, on that ever winding road in search of others.

But where to start?

Do I begin this tale with the whispers, or try and explain it with what I do know of us?

Being a man of science I feel it must be the latter. Picking up my pen I take a deep breath. There is no turning back from this. If I am to do this I must tell the whole story. I write down *A New Dawn* and underline it, searching for more words. And they arrive. Writing furiously I manage to fill three pages with science and my own musings. There will be a healthy amount of speculation in the coming pages because this is all I have.

Upon finishing the first chapter I dot the last full

stop and smile. I'd like to call this book *A memoir of an Immortal Man*, but I already know this will not be. Apinya has told me the title of a book he has read many times, the book I have just finished the first chapter of. It will be called *Immortal - a memoir*.

I wonder what would happen to this world Apinya comes from if I decided not to write this book. It is an interesting concept regarding the travel of time and the effects someone like Apinya could have on the world.

Opening the desk drawer I slip the journal inside and proceed to get ready for class. Today is my first History lecture and I am looking forward to it. Having lived through the history I teach, I can give a first hand account of what it was like back then. This usually opens up lively debates with students, gets them involved, makes them have to think, form their own opinions, as opposed to just listening to their Professor drone on and on. I've also found getting students involved with the class works wonders for them retaining information instead of sleeping through it.

Today's lecture will be more of an introduction of myself and the forthcoming year.

When I arrive at the class I see one student is already here, Apie Chester.

'Good morning Mr. Chester,' I say, passing him on

the front row and putting my satchel down on the desk in front of the blackboard.

Apinya smiles at me.

'What? What on earth are you grinning at young man?'

He shakes his head, 'Nothing really. A few weeks ago I sat in the front row of a theatre and watched you take a lecture which had the entire room packed to the gills.'

I frown, 'Should you be talking of my future? Perhaps I will stop teaching and never return to class again. What then would happen to this memory you just called upon?'

Apinya shrugs, 'Sorry William but it doesn't work like that. It has already happened which means it will always happen.'

'And what about free will? If what you say is correct, this means we live our lives not really making any decision for ourselves. It is all preordained, we are merely puppets in a show, unable to make any real decisions for ourselves.'

He laughs, shaking his head, 'Why did you choose to wear that jacket this morning William? Was there some preordained force making you chose it? Was your hand forced?'

'No.'

'No. Through our lives we make decisions but once we have made them we cannot unmake them.'

'But you talk of me teaching at a future date in my life. I haven't made that decision yet, therefore I am able to change the outcome.'

Again another shake of the head, 'Not so. Just like I will always watch you deliver that lecture a few weeks ago, you will always decide to be at the front of the theatre delivering it. You can't change the past but equally, you have complete control over your own future. There was never a 1958 where I was not here. Do you understand? There was never a version of right now where we weren't having this discussion.'

'And what if I decide to throw out my memoir, discontinue it and burn in the grate the pages I have written?'

Apinya looks hard at me and then sighs. 'You know it was you who taught me this, when I was just a boy. You explained the semantics of time travel and how what has gone before cannot be altered because it is already history.'

'Ok, ok,' I say, holding up my hands, 'I submit. I will enjoy understanding this one day so that I might impart my wisdom upon you.'

'That's the spirit.'

'Tell me though, for fun, what was I teaching in this future theatre packed to the gills?'

Apinya laughs, 'You were talking about The Divine, about the memoir you penned in 1958. Professor Crawford has become the leading expert on all things Divine.'

'Divine? What is Divine?'

'This is what you call the people you write about in your memoir.'

And because he has just told me of this, it will always be the name I choose. I cannot change it because I never did. I like the sound of this name though, The Divine, and make a mental note to add it into my opening chapter when I arrive home later.

As other students begin to make their way into class and take their seats, I squat next to Apinya's table. 'Tell me something. Something I have always wondered. Why is it you came to me, revealing yourself back in the trenches? I've always wondered and never asked you then.'

'You needed to meet Uncle Eric. Without a friendship blossoming between you two, your memoir, my childhood, countless future lives would be lost. One action leads onto the next, like falling dominoes.'

'But where does the trail of falling dominoes end?'

Apinya smiles, 'End is the wrong word William.

Lead would be a better fit. They will lead you to The Phoenix Committee and a man called Victor Morris.'

'Victor Morris? And when will I meet this particular man?'

'You've already met him William. Many many years ago.'

I rest my hand on his shoulder and give it a squeeze. The last time he was here was to make sure Eric and I met, this time so that I write this memoir, but why? This goes against his own logic. If I always wrote this book then he needn't interfere because I always wrote it.

I stand up and nod at a few students taking their seats. Looking back at the young man who I know as Apinya Chesterfield but who his classmates will call Apie, I smile. The future is set. There is nothing I can do about this because it always happened that way. There are no alternate timelines, no forks in the road. What is to happen in my life is a memory already in Apinya's. One day I will explain this to a young boy who will then travel back in time and meet me during the Great War. A few years later he will travel through time once again and introduce himself to me at a faculty get-together.

My head hurts. Back in the trenches I knew he was not from these parts. He confided in me then. But now…now I must write my story, but not only mine. I must write Eric's story and to do that I need to go back to his beginning. To his first life. One shrouded in death. One shrouded in blood.

'Good morning class,' I say as the last seat is taken. 'I will be your professor for the time being as Mr. Waybridge has taken ill. My name is William and I'd like for you to join me on a journey back in time…'

Chapter Ten

THE DIVINE

There have been many times during my life when I have questioned my existence. In the thirteen hundreds, once William Wallace was, to all intent and purposes dead, I felt a great burden lift from my shoulders. The man I was brought into this life as was dead and now I had the freedom to forge a new path of my own.

Back then I was an educated man for the times but there were questions I sought answers to and still do. Over the ages I have met very few like me and apart from Eric none were keen to join me on my voyage of discovery.

The question of what we are, as a species, is the big one.

Do I have it wrong and are we really 'Gods' or 'Angels' put here to protect mankind? Being a man of science I prefer to shy away from this notion. I do not possess a halo, my savagery in past lives would not do well in earning me one either, and if my feathered wings were ever going to sprout out of my back I would have thought after eight hundred years they would have made an appearance.

As a scientist I rely upon evidence to draw my conclusions from but so far there has been none. Indeed, before Eric came along there had been just two others I had come across over the years who I believed to be Divine.

I met the charismatic Count de Saint-Germain, a man who courted the limelight in society circles all over Europe, in the eighteenth century. I had the pleasure of dining with him in 1760 while working in Paris as a science professor. Before then I had heard the rumours, that there was a man whose skin does not age. The man was well read, well-travelled, charming, easy going and had a great scientific mind. We spoke for hours about the art of alchemy, a subject which the Count was most enthusiastic about, but when I pressed more about immortality the man clammed up.

There are of course many myths surrounding this man and there have been many sightings of the Count up and down the ages. The Count spoke many languages and we conversed in several over dinner. Later, after our meal we had agreed to meet for a nightcap at his room to talk some more. I wanted to persuade him that we may help each other in one another's work but he had left Paris quickly during our interlude.

Had I spooked him, having almost confessed to him that he was not the only immortal man walking the Earth? Maybe I'll never know as I never met him again.

A few months later, while dining with the high society set I had managed to embroil myself within, I bore witness to a fantastic tale told by an elderly Countess, Madame de Pompadour, the then ageing mistress of Louis XV. She said she had known Count de Saint-Germain in Venice in the early 1700s and upon meeting him this time around she had been curious how it appeared he hadn't seemed to age a day in the fifty years since their first meeting. When she asked the man if it had in fact been his father she had known all those years ago the Count replied, 'No Madame, I myself was living in Venice at the end of the last and beginning of this century and I had the honour to pay you court then.'

'Forgive me but that is impossible,' the Countess had responded, 'The Count Saint-Germain I knew all that time ago was at least forty-five years old, and you at the outside are that age at present.'

The Countess then told us that he had smiled and replied, 'Madame I am very old.'

When she questioned him further, stating that he must be nearly one hundred years old, the Count had told her that such things were impossible and then proceeded to convince her that he was in fact the same man that she knew fifty years previously in Venice.

In this day and age living to the age of one hundred, for a mortal man, is possible. I add a year upon my own age every summer. Maybe the Count does not. I might understand why this is when we do not age and I only wish I had met with him some more on my travels, but as my journeying took me across to the Americas to learn the native tongues, hoping to learn also of men or women like myself, St-Germain stayed in Europe and continued to court the Parisian high society. The man popped up throughout the rest of the eighteenth century and in writer Albert Vandam's memoir 'An Englishman in Paris 1843-1903' Vandam claimed to have met a man who bore a striking resemblance to Count de Saint-Germain but who went by the name of Major Fraser.

He wrote: he called himself Major Fraser, lived alone and never alluded to his family. Moreover he was lavish with money, though the source of his fortune remained a mystery to everyone. He possessed marvellous knowledge of all countries in Europe at all periods. His memory was absolutely incredible and, curiously enough, he often gave his hearers to understand that he had acquired his learning elsewhere than from books. Many is the time he told me, with a strange smile, that he was certain he had known Nero, had spoken with Dante and so on.'

Now, if these claims were true and St-Germain had known the Roman Emperor Nero then that would mean he would be closing in on two thousand years old. I could speculate forever about this man I met just once and tie him in with a whole manner of 'miracles' which are now quite frankly considered Gospel. I only wonder why though, when I questioned him on immortality he was so reserved where in other documented instances the man has seemingly gushed about his secrets?

Perhaps one day I will have the pleasure of meeting with this intriguing gentleman again and ask him this.

Another who I found was the same as me came as

quite a shock because I had loved and cared for this person centuries earlier. There had been a point where we had been inseparable but as our lives steered us in different directions we lost contact. I had no idea they were Divine and in hindsight, I probably should have.

This person repaid the love and care I gave to them by accusing me of betraying them and then burying me inside an iron tomb for forty years until I managed to escape. I believe they were hoping I would remain there for eternity.

It was a nightmarish time those four decades of solitary but it taught me something new about my cell's regeneration, being that if starved of food and water my body will slowdown and hibernate. I was able to conduct a medical examination on myself periodically and found my heart was beating at a steady two beats a day thus delivering oxygen to my organs much slower than usual. Days, weeks, months might have passed during those dark times and will have felt like minutes as the connections in my brain also slowed to a near standstill. I was conscious but my mind was sluggish. This time of confinement became a time of reflection, to try and understand more what kept my body going and my body's limits.

It took me forty solid years to scratch my way out

of my tomb which was in fact a cast iron coffin of sorts. Then I found myself buried deep in a forest in Scotland. By the time I reached civilisation again instead of embarking on a trail of vengeance I made the decision to simply continue on my quest to find more of the Divine.

I imagine my path will one day cross with my captor, and in writing this they will undoubtedly learn of my escape from the prison they entombed me inside. Let me just say that when our paths do again cross I will not be as kind as to bury their head still attached to their body.

Eric Chesterfield, my brother, my companion, I met simply by chance. It appears for all my searching it is chance which leads me to my quarry, and in finding Eric there was no exception.

Having studied science and medicine in several lives, I have been accustomed to being able to settle into any community when I grow weary of my travels. Dr William Steel was one such incarnation in which I felt like a rest.

It was the early 1900s and I had spent the best part of a century travelling around the globe. I decided it was time to relax for twenty or thirty years, to stop obsessing and searching for my kind, to forget about the meaning of the Divine's existence and simply live my life.

I chose a small Cumbrian town on the cusp of the Pennines to set up shop as the town's Doctor. My credentials were good, I had studied medicine ten years earlier at King's college and so in this life I was not required to forge my qualifications as I have previously had to.

Roaming through this life with infinite years ahead of me I have found education a fantastic stimulant and I have often excelled in many subjects. I am a professor of biology and natural history; I am fluent in twenty languages and can manage to hold conversations in another fifteen. Periodic history I have lived through and so have an eyewitness account which makes teaching about it simply a trip down memory lane. The subjects which interest have generally been the ones which might aid me in my search. Medicine was a given. To understand my own physiology I needed to understand that of my closest ancestor which is the Homo-sapien.

When the post of village Doctor arose in the small town of Kendle, I was happy to fill it and so I set up shop. Not only am I fluent in many languages but my dialects and accents in and around Britain are reasonably accurate. The broad northern tongue I slipped into with ease won over the locals and I soon became one of them.

Small town gossip usually runs rife anywhere in the world and Kendle was no exception. Again, it was simply by chance one day that I overheard a couple of the old boys chatting in my surgery's reception area.

'You can't trust that family, keeping themselves to themselves like they do, living all the way out in the sticks on that farm and only coming into town for supplies and for church on Sundays.'

'Yep. That nephew of theirs I haven't seen for ten years although his uncle, old Benjamin, assured me last week that Richard still stays with them.'

If it hadn't been for the next remark I most probably would not have stopped dead in my tracks.

'Old lady Vera said she can remember the family when she was a girl, and even then she said she remembers Richard Woodley around, toiling the land and breaking in horses.'

'As a boy? I'd have not thought him over thirty-five now.'

'Well that's the thing, and old George Hillsop the town elder will confirm it, Richard hasn't appeared to age a day in three decades. He still appears in his mid-thirties now.'

This sent my adrenaline bouncing around in my

veins. It was a similar story to that told by the Parisian countess a century earlier. The recluse Richard Woodley was one of the Divine.

In the following months I tried to get close to the man but found it impossible. He did not leave the Woodley farm and they seldom received guests. It wasn't until old Benjamin Woodley died that Richard ventured off the family farm to attend his grandson's funeral.

At the funeral Richard was called out, branded first an imposter and then the devil, and I believe had I not intervened, knowing what I now know about my friend, there would have been many mortal deaths that day.

Richard fled the town he had called home with the family he had reared for one hundred and fifty years and soon after so too did Dr William Steel. Having once again stumbled upon one of my own I knew I would have to start again, to assume a fresh identity and continue my search for more people like me.

And so my search continued, but being a member of such an obscure and hidden ethnic group has been like looking for the proverbial needle…physically we appear just like man. It is only on the cellular level where there are differences. We once were man, before our 'awakening' as I like to call the moment our cells begin to regenerate rapidly.

Upon writing I am around seven hundred and forty years old, and in that time I have discovered only three others like me. Although it stands to reason there must be more, we hide well in plain sight and this leads me to the second big question I have no way of finding the answer to.

How many do the Divine number?

We are not mythical creatures created by God to roam the earth. And even if we were, which God would have created us? From vast experience on my travels I have learned that the Christian God is just one of thousands of Gods worshiped the world over.

The scientist and evolutionist inside me shuns this very notion and concentrates on the facts. We are born to mortal parents and at some point in our lives the rapid cell regeneration process kicks in which stops us ageing and heals us whenever we are hurt. But, as fantastic as it is, is it only cell regeneration where our powers lie?

My thoughts return to my old acquaintance Count Saint-Germain who could quite possibly have been around at the time of Christ and also be able to pull off Christ's crucifixion and subsequent resurrection. Stories passed down through the ages have always had a habit of becoming legend and even 'gospel'. Eric has also had people write stories based upon him throughout history, indeed there is a certain Irish novelist who Eric befriended in the small town of Whitby in the late nineteenth century who has a lot to answer for. But that, as they say, is another story.

Chapter Eleven

THE BATTLE OF THE RED FOX

Sometimes I have an urge to revisit the person I was back at the beginning. The savage warrior still resides inside me. The cumbersome, sometimes shy professor who towers over his peers in stature is only one side of me. It has been many centuries since I have wielded a sword, but I believe if circumstances presented themselves where I needed such an instrument to fight with, I would do so with ease.

This afternoon after class I wrote the second and third chapters of my memoir, adding in the name I use for our kind, The Divine. This put me back in the skin of Wallace. After the writing was complete I could not shake an anger which came from deep inside unforgotten memories. Nessie. The little girl I promised I would return for and never did. How different her life may have been if not for my selfishness. My little Nessie. A character in the life of William Wallace that history forgot.

Once these chapters were finished I couldn't think of anything else. I am no writer. I have never tried to craft a story and my mind feels stagnant now, void of anything to commit to paper.

I headed out for an afternoon stroll. My classes were finished for the day and I thought it would be good to get a bit of air, clear the mind, and so I just began walking, reliving my lives in my head. I often wonder about the children I have fathered down the ages. Children who grew up and would lose their father in their twenties. I can recall every one of their faces, put a name to each of their smiles.

A few years ago a grandson I never knew was murdered. The story made the national news because he was one of many victims whose life was cut short by the killer. I attended the funeral and shook hands with the grieving father, my once son, William. He didn't recognise me. Perhaps had he not been blinded by sorrow he might have noticed how I resembled a man who he once doted on as a child.

His mother, my once wife, did recognise me though. She was old by now, half blind and with the onset of dementia poor woman, but when she shook my hand, heard my voice, she knew it was me, returning when she thought she'd lost me forever. I never told her of my longevity, but after three decades together there will have been things she had noticed. Spend every day with somebody and you do not see them age, but you will recognise yourself ageing. The wrinkles on her face became more pronounced, her hair started turning grey, her body changed, skin became looser and her memory was not all that it once was. Margret was fifty-three years old when I left my life with her and I walked away looking exactly as I had the day she had met me as a young woman.

When I shook her hand at our grandson's funeral she knew it was me. She even whispered my name and squeezed my hand that little bit tighter. She knew.

Memories such as this eat me from the inside. Man has three score years and ten to live their life, I only have thirty years before I must leave and abandon the people I chose to make a life with. The alternative, to stay, always ends in blood, ends in the town turning against you, family, friends, everyone you love believing you not divine, but cursed.

I feel I may repeat myself in the writing of this

memoir, but that I cannot help. My life has been a repeat of itself time and time again. My thirty years is never long enough. Perhaps that is really the reason I search for others, so that I might one day have a companion, a love, who I will not need to leave to save myself, watching them die at the end of their three score years and ten.

It is beginning to get dark. Autumn in England is beautiful but the day does not last long.

I should head back, but I am enjoying this, aimlessly walking across the city, my past lives like sullen companions replaying themselves in my mind. The warrior and the lover, the historian and the scientist, I am all of them and I am none of them. These are but roles I have played in my many lives. Skins I am able to fit into when the need calls for it.

In need of refreshment, I open the door of a public house and walk to the bar, ordering a glass of ale.

'Would you like some nuts with that?' The barkeep asks and I agree, handing him a few more coins and sitting down at the end of the bar on a stool.

There are fifteen other men sat in the pub, some talking quietly at tables, others minding their own business at the bar where I have taken up residence.

'Haven't seen you around these parts before, guv'nor.'

I smile, 'I was just out for a walk and got a thirst.'

The barkeeper nods at this, polishing the ale pump in front of me with his bar towel.

'Are you local?'

I laugh, perhaps a little too loud as this causes a table of men in the corner to turn their heads, 'I'm not sure, where are we?'

'Tower 'amlets sir.'

I shake my head, checking my wristwatch. It is approaching half seven in the evening. 'It would appear I've walked across half of London this afternoon.'

'Not to worry, there's a tube stop just down the road, that'll get you back to where you're supposed to be. Where are you coming from?'

'The University of London. I'm a Professor there.'

'Ohhh, la-d-dah. A professor is it? What do you teach?'

'History and Medicine.'

The barkeep is still smiling but I watch as his eyes harden. It is a look I have seen many times before. A look of revulsion. I do not belong here. Or rather, a professor of History and Medicine from a University does not. I have drunk wine with kings and gulped ale with paupers in my time. There really is no difference when in the company of your peers. But just as that pauper would not be seen drinking at the King's table and the King would not be seen splashing ale down his gullet in a dockside drinking hole, I do not belong here.

I check my watch again, drinking my ale in one gulp.

'Perhaps it's time I should be making my way home,' I say cheerfully enough.

'Nah, don't be silly *Professor*, it's not every day we have someone of your standing lowering themselves to our level, stay for another,' the barkeep says, already pouring me a second glass of beer.

The men at the table in the corner have now started whispering between themselves, looking across the room at the clueless professor. Who on earth does he think he is, coming into *their* pub?

I thank the barkeep for the second drink and offer my hand, 'William.'

'Charlie, pleased to meet you sir.'

'Might I buy you a drink seeing as how I am staying for a second one?'

Charlie grins, 'Got to put some pennies in the till, William.'

'You buying?' One of the men from the corner table calls across the room. I ignore this. I can feel the whole pub staring at the "rich" Professor now.

'Cheers sir,' Charlie offers, holding up his glass.

I touch his glass rim with mine and nod.

'You deaf or what?'

'Probably not wanting to associate with the likes of us.'

'Is that right?'

Here we go. The reason I should not have walked into this establishment living the life of a University Professor.

I turn to the men, still smiling, always remaining calm on the exterior while beneath the surface I can feel that warrior sharpening his broadsword.

'I do apologise gentlemen but I have only limited monies on my person. Perhaps next time?'

Before I can turn back to the bar, one of the men says, 'Is he mugging us off?'

'I think he might be, you know. Coming in here flashing his money about. He'll buy Charlie a drink but not us, why not?'

I sigh. Somethings never change. Whether it be sat around a campfire drinking mead in the 1500s, or stood at a bar in occupied France during the 1940s, there will always be those groups of men who prey on the seemingly weak. I glance back over my shoulder at these men, hard men who have hard lives. They put in a real day's work. They know their place, get paid very little but work and sweat for that money, and now some city Professor poof walks into *their* pub and is refusing to buy them a drink. Who does he think he is?

'I think he's taking liberties, Pete.'

'Oh without a doubt. Maybe we should relieve him of whatever he *does* have in his pockets?'

At that moment the pub door opens and Charlie the barkeep finds an excuse to go in the back. Three boys enter, each one well built, hair combed into the teddy boy quiff, the dying breed of the 50's rock culture inherited from America.

'Carl, come here boy.'

The three walk over to the far table, 'What's up Uncle Pete?'

'Him,' Uncle Pete says, pointing in my direction. 'Throwing his money around but refuses to buy us hard working men a drink.'

The three greased up children who are barely out of their teens, look my way.

I smile, holding up a hand in greeting as they approach.

'You need to leave William,' I hear Charlie hiss from behind the bar somewhere.

'This true?'

I turn in my seat, finishing my drink and standing up.

'No, it's not true, I tried explaining…'

'Shut up.' One of the three shouts, pushing me back, into the bar.

I can feel him under the surface now, ready to erupt. Had this been centuries earlier these children would already be dead on the floor. Times change though. I won't retaliate.

Behind the Teds, Pete and his gang watch, sneering, laughing, joking at my expense. That'll teach the poof, coming into *our* pub and snubbing us.

'That there is my uncle. Why wouldn't you buy him a drink?'

I shake my head. There is no talking these young men down. They're with their crowd, it is all about maintaining their image amongst their gang.

'I don't have the money your uncle speaks of.'

'So you're calling him a liar?'

I smile, 'Just mis-informed.'

As the fist flies through the air towards my face, I marvel at how predictable some people are, lowering my head so that his knuckles connect with the top of my head. I hear the crack of his bones and watch as he staggers back, clutching the broken fingers.

'What the fuck did you just do,' the second one shouts, taking off his belt in one fluid motion and swinging it around in front of him. Once upon a time we had a weapon called a mace, heavy wooden handle with chain and a spiked iron ball on the end. This weapon was deadly when it found its target. This boy's belt buckle is not.

As he swings his 1950's style mace through the air, I veer to the right punching him hard in the nose and then following with a jab to the third Teddy Boy's throat. With the three young men incapacitated, I feel now would be a good time to leave.

'Oy, oy, where do you think you're going?' Pete and his friends call across the room. I ignore them, exiting the pub and walking across the carpark, waiting for this particular battle to spill out onto the street.

Before I've time to turn, I hear the scream as the door bursts open and the four men sat in the corner minding their own business before the University professor entered their domain mugging them off, leave the pub.

'Get here, we're not done big boy,' Pete calls across.

I need to stifle the warrior which is fighting to be unleashed. This isn't a time when fights can be finished with men dead in a ditch, there would be repercussions. How long would it take for police to find the tall, young University Professor? And then I would have to leave once more, an identity wasted because I could not control myself.

'I'm not fighting you men,' I say as they approach. 'This is a mistake.'

'You're damn right, sonny. That was my nephew you floored. Not to worry though, my brother, his father, is on his way from the docks with a couple of lads.'

I nod, watching as the three Teddy Boys make their way out of the pub behind Uncle Pete and his friends, each holding a bar stool in their hands.

'How about you and I fight?' I ask. 'Just us. Afterwards the winner is rewarded a beer and we shake hands?'

Pete laughs at the very thought as he approaches, fists bunched up into white balls.

I take my jacket off, folding it and placing it on the low wall which makes up the perimeter of the carpark.

'All right then,' I whisper, watching as two Teddy Boys produce knives. I can't use them. I hurt these men and I start right back from the beginning.

Pete runs at me swinging his arms and I wait until he is about to land a blow before pivoting and pushing him over the wall. He lands on his back, legs in the air as two of his friends both approach me with the three Teddy Boys right behind them. Five against one, a coward's fight.

They stop just as I clench my own fists.

Laughing, they point behind me, 'You've had it now.'

I turn my head and watch a small van speeding up the road. No doubt the brother and his friends from the dock.

'Hi William, need some help?'

Walking around the corner I see Apinya, smiling, always smiling, always laughing, that carefree crooked smile which was inherited from Eric.

'Apinya you need to leave,' I cry out to him.

He shakes his head, 'Nah, you know that never happened.'

'Let me guess, I sent you?'

'You know the answer to that already. You've got a lot to thank yourself for one day.'

'What the hell is this?' One of them calls out, 'You got a little chinky friend to try and even the odds?'

Apinya looks at me and raises his eyebrows, mouthing the word '*chinky?*' and shaking his head.

A beer bottle is thrown, narrowly missing Apinya's head.

'You ready William?'

I nod, 'You?'

He grins and charges at the five men, striking one and then another, then another with lightning fast punches. I turn my attention to the men piling out of the van. There are four of them, each holding a weapon of some description, metal pipe, crowbar, another with a length of chain.

'Not so tough now, are you?' One of them says.

I throw myself at him, smashing his jaw with all the strength I can muster and watching him slump to the ground. Picking up his crowbar, I move onto the next one, shattering his knees. The last two think better of it and drop their weapons, hands up, retreating back to the van just as I feel the sharp stinging of the blade in my side. I turn, gripping the Teddy Boy by the throat and squeezing, aware I cannot see this to the end. A death would mean a new beginning. I throw the boy across the carpark, watching as Apinya is hit in the head with a brick. He drops to the floor and I run over kicking his attacker square in the chest and dropping to my knees.

'Apinya, are you ok?'

His eyes open and he nods as I feel the shadow loom over me.

Before I can turn, Apinya's hand reaches out and I watch as he takes the assailant by the arm. No force, no deadly blow, he merely brushes his fingers against the man's wrist for half a second and the man drops to the floor unconscious.

Sirens.

The local plod have been alerted, probably by Charlie the barkeep.

I lift Apinya up onto his feet, 'Can you walk?'

'Yeah, I'm alright.'

'Come on, let's get out of here.'

We make our way out of the carpark and head down the road towards Mile End tube station.

'How did you know I'd be here, Apinya?'

'Are you kidding me? I've waited over a decade to fight with you in the battle of The Red Fox.'

I look back and, sure enough the pub is called The Red Fox. It is then I realise something, understand the connection Apinya has with me. He lives his life waiting for moments where we come together, but one day I will meet a scared little boy and it will be my turn to know *his* future, to be the one already with this relationship, this connection.

Chapter Twelve

VLAD

Theories are all I really have. As a man of science it is infuriating to know that although the data must be out there somewhere, it has been almost impossible to collect. To discover more about my kind I need test subjects, and as I mentioned in a previous chapter I have met only a few other members of my species in my life. Out of them, my dear friend Eric has been a constant in my life for the majority of this century, and I have learned so much from him. It is Eric and the amazing abilities he rather reluctantly possesses I would now like to talk about.

Eric was born Vlad III, Prince of Wallachia in

1431 in Eastern Europe. In the winter of 1476 Vlad, or Eric as he is known these days, was beheaded by the Turks and his head was sent back to Constantinople and put on display to the public, impaled on a stake. Quite the grizzly ending for a man who, during his life, was rumoured to have slain 100,000 people, but as with the demise of Sir William Wallace a century earlier, it is possible to survive a beheading if in fact it is not you losing your head.

Eric first discovered his ability to heal in battle. On many occasions he has recounted the blow of the sabre to his left collarbone and him collapsing at the feet of his men, only to rise again and fight on, and it is my belief that our first 'death' is what holds the key to our eternity.

Man's body heals. Cut him and he will bleed, but given time wounds close and he will live to fight another day. When presented with that fatal blow our body's cells change or rather something kick starts inside us, speeding up our rate of healing (rapid regeneration) and with this destroying the ageing gene which leads to our inevitable immortality.

When Man's cells die they do so having copied themselves over and over again, but each copy is inferior to the last. In time the generations of cells begin to break down and this is how ageing occurs. The blood thins, the immune system weakens, making man more susceptible to disease, hair pigment is lost, sight weakens, and these are but a few symptoms of old age, of the cells breaking down.

Our cells do not produce inferior copies. Our bodies are, in effect, frozen in time. After that initial trigger point when the body begins its rapid cell regeneration, we become much stronger. I can bench press 900lb, and while this does not make me a record breaker, I am a scientist not a professional bodybuilder. Once the Divine cells have woken up I believe their density greatens. We are stronger, faster, and heal at an alarming rate, and until I met Eric I believed that was the extent of my kind's abilities.

My thoughts go back to no man's land and Eric appearing from nowhere, out of thin air. He has the ability to bend light around his body, something I cannot even begin to understand. And invisibility is not Eric's only trick. The first time he showed me how he could 'will' himself into the air I was astounded. When I questioned how he was able to do this, Eric explained that it had something to do with the sun, like plants photosynthesising, his body collects energy from the sun's rays and when harnessed and dispersed he is able to move through the air.

'The air feels heavy against me and with this I am able to manipulate my direction.'

I did not understand it then and I do not now but although so far I have not discovered the answers, there still must be reason behind these feats. As mystical as it appears when watching man take off into the air, there is science behind it, hiding, bending its own light around the answers which I search for.

Far Eastern cultures believe in Karma, ying and yang, that every action has an equal and opposite reaction and with Eric's power lurks a much darker side, the hunger. Eric himself calls his thirst for blood and the onslaught of symptoms beforehand, the beast. I, as always, am a little more sceptical. I do not imagine a beast lurks within my friend but I have seen how Eric turns when he does not quench his thirst. Instead of listing the theories I have regarding 'the beast' I will instead tell you a story.

In 1890 on the Yorkshire coast in the seaside town of Whitby, Eric's beast once more rose and made its way out into the night to seek its fill. Having prowled the dark night's streets, the beast found its victim and pounced, taking the man by the throat, stifling his screams, and carrying them both up into the air, landing in the graveyard of Whitby castle which overlooks the town.

The man the beast chose for that night's fill was an Irish writer called Abraham, and strangely enough he did not appear frightened in this ordeal. After feeding from the man Eric did not flee. He was curious as to why there was no fear.

Abraham had answered, 'This has been the most deadly and enchanting experience, and although of course I feared for my life, my inquisitive nature overrode any fear I might have had.'

Eric saw something in Abraham that night. He had spent his life either embracing the beast which led to the massacre of thousands in his first life, or suppressing it, which led to a life of constant craving, but one thing he had never done was talk about his need for the blood, until that night.

He found he was able to tell his story to his would-be victim, and Abraham listened. Eric told him everything, from his time many lives ago as the Wallachia prince, to present day lurking in the shadows trying to survive. When they parted they shook hands and Abraham thanked Eric for his story. Seven years later, after some research into Eric's origins, the Irish writer who had come so close to death, released a novel which romanticised everything about the beast Eric still fights to this day. That novel is now part of literary history, its primary character one of popular culture's best loved villains.

In 1476 Vlad III, Prince of Walachia died. He was posthumously dubbed Vlad the Impaler, because of his penchant for impaling his enemies and drinking their blood to instil fear in his enemies. During his life he was a member of the House of Draculseti and had also been known by his patronymic name, Dracula.

Chapter Thirteen

AFTERMATH

'Are you alright Apinya?' I ask, handing him a coffee mug containing a splash of whiskey. 'Sorry, I haven't got around to buying some glasses.'

Apinya nods, 'It'll still taste the same,' he says, toasting the air and taking a sip.

I drop down into the armchair across from him and sigh. It has been many years since I've gone into battle, and I must say it is what I think I needed to blow those cobwebs away. I feel alive. My senses are sharpened, my hands won't stop bloody shaking from the adrenaline still coursing through my system. For a moment back there the warrior was resurrected.

I look across at the boy and smile. He had waited a decade for us to join forces and go to war with a bunch of local thugs.

'How are you feeling?'

'Isn't that the same as asking if I'm alright?' He laughs, 'Don't worry about me William, I've been through far worse.'

'Tell me about that?'

Apinya shakes his head, closing his eyes and taking another sip of his whiskey. 'Oh William,' he says smiling, 'Always wanting more, always asking questions. Can we not just sit in peace and enjoy our whiskies? I have wondered what today would feel like many times since you told me of our fight outside The Red Fox. The first time you mentioned it you were helping me try to control these…' he wiggles his fingers as he says this, eyes still closed, as if talking more to himself than to me.

'When was this?'

'2003 at Chesterfield Manor, I was nine or ten and then I was nine again.'

I shake my head. What on earth does that mean?

Apinya opens his eyes and notes my confusion, 'When I arrived at Chesterfield Manor I was nine years old and I spent a year there with Uncle Eric, and you, Alan, and of course Sophie…' He trails off and then, 'I must be tired William, I've just mentioned someone who will not be born for a number of years.'

I sit up in my chair, 'Who? Sophie? Who is she?'

Apinya laughs, 'She's my best friend, she's the one woman I will always love, and she's no concern of yours…yet,' he winks and I shake my head in mock annoyance.

'Always giving me little snippets of information and then cutting me off. Can you imagine how frustrating this is for me?'

'Of course I can. When I was younger I had many questions but you would always do the same. I couldn't tell you who started this little game of ours, whether it was me meeting you in the trenches or you meeting me as a boy, but I'll give you that, it is frustrating.'

'Tell me about what you did to that thug who you sent to the ground by simply touching his wrist. How did you do that Apinya?'

'How about you tell me about the book? How is it coming along?'

I let out a sigh. I have no more words. Three chapters I've managed and now my mind is blank. 'Not well. Perhaps I'll revisit it another time.'

Apinya smiles, 'Perhaps you just need a little inspiration.'

I nod, 'What would you suggest?'

'First a top up ehh?' He says, waving his empty coffee cup in my direction.

I agree to his terms and reach for the bottle on the table between us. As I move to pour, Apinya reaches out for my hand and I am frozen. Static fills my ears and as my vision begins to tunnel the last thing I hear, like a faint whisper on the breeze, are his words, 'See you on the other side, Doc.'

Darkness.

The buzzing in my head still there and when I open my eyes I find myself lying on my back looking up at the clear blue sky beyond the leafy tree branches affording me shade. I hear voices. Muffled at first but then I make out the words.

'And you sure it is now? Would it not have been better to show him after he wrote the book?'

Sitting up, the muffled silhouettes come into focus and there stands Apinya, a huge grin on his face, and Eric, leaning against the tree smoking one of his god awful cigars.

'Hey Doc, nice of you to join us.'

I sit up, feeling the cool dew between my fingers from the grass beneath them.

'Eric?'

He nods, smiling and reaching down to help me up onto my feet.

'You know, when Pin told me his plan to bring you here from when you're coming from I had my reservations, but the boy won't be told.'

'As stubborn as a mule you said Uncle Eric. Now wherever would I get that from?'

Eric shakes his head, and rolls his eyes at me, wrapping his arms around me, 'Cocky as well. Always bloody right. Come on Doc, let's head up to the house.'

Both Eric and Apinya start moving off up the road towards Chesterfield Manor.

'Wait, what, stop, both of you just stop right there. What the hell is going on here? One moment I'm sat in my cottage with you Apinya, and now poof...here I am at Chesterfield Manor. Have we teleported?'

Both Eric and Apinya look at each other and start laughing.

'Jesus Doc, this isn't an episode of Star Trek...'

'He's coming from the fifties, Eric.'

'Oh shit. Sorry, ignore that.'

'Star Trek?' I say.

'It's just something which will run on television and they make a bunch of movies. It doesn't matter, forget I mentioned it. Just come up to the house and we'll explain everything.'

I follow them up. Eric and Apinya walking ahead, arms around each other, chatting quietly to themselves just out of earshot. As we walk I look back at the tree I woke up underneath and there are two things which I did not notice upon my waking. The first is a rope swing dangling down from a high branch, the second a headstone just off to the right, out of the shade of the canopy and in the sun.

'Is young Alan here?' I ask as we reach the door.

Eric turns and shakes his head, 'Not so young anymore William. You're not where you think you are. You didn't just leave a few weeks ago for your post at London University. Come on, we'd like to chat about your work.'

'My work?'

'Your book.'

We walk into the house and everything looks different. The kitchen countertop is some sort of black stone, there is a work surface in the middle of the room with four stools up against it, like a bar top, even the kettle is different and appears to be made of glass.

'Eric, what's going on? Why has everything changed here? The headstone underneath the oak tree, this kitchen…is that kettle made out of glass?'

Apinya bursts out laughing, 'Don't sweat the small stuff William…'

'Sweat what?'

'Sorry, it's just a phrase.'

'Both of you stop. Where am I?'

Eric shakes his head, 'Not where, Doc, when. And that question will be answered in due course.'

I follow them both out of the kitchen and down the corridor. On the walls are paintings and photographs I've seen a hundred times before. The evolution of the Chesterfield clan. Eric the forever constant, his clothes and hairstyle changing but the face always remaining the same age, the same crooked smile beaming back. As I pass photos I have seen many times before, I watch as, before my eyes, Alan Chesterfield grows up, his University graduation, wedding day, Alan standing outside a building yard with a huge sign behind him displaying the name *Chesterfield Homes*. Further on down the wall I watch the young man I spoke to only a few days ago, grow into an older man, hair receding and whitening, face hardening until he is stood around the kitchen table with Eric, a young girl with piercing green eyes, a young boy who is quite obviously Apinya, and…and me. There I stand smiling with the rest of them, a future me stood in front of a toddler.

Apinya moves to my side and smiles, 'Remember that Christmas Eric?' He says, touching the glass and running his finger down the little girl's face affectionately.

'Sophie?' I ask him, and he nods.

'Do you recognise that smile?'

I laugh. Of course I do, it is a Chesterfield trait, the crooked smile, and anyway she is the spitting image of her father only without the cigar stuck in the side of her mouth.

I turn to Eric, 'Your daughter?

He nods and beckons me into his study.

As we walk in it is nice to see some things don't change much. Eric's study hasn't differed since I was first invited here in 1930. The furniture has changed but his desk still stands by the south facing window, the open fireplace still sits in the opposite corner, yes, the place has an air of familiarity to it.

Eric opens his arms to allow me to pass him at the doorway and as I walk into the study a man I'd put in his early fifties stands up and approaches, infectious cheery smile and bright eyes. 'William, may I introduce Robert Macmillan.'

Chapter Fourteen

1607

It had been three hundred and two years since one of history's greatest escapes, and to this day I sometimes think about the man who took my place at my execution. His name was Donnchadh Mór, which translated from Gaelic meant Big Duncan, a man who like me, towered over his peers, a farmer and a father who fought many battles by my side against the English. Men would often comment of our likeness and when we wore beards the resemblance was uncanny. After our betrayal and defeat by the Scottish nobles at Falkirk I was branded an outlaw and so went into hiding, travelling to France to rally support from the French King. Knowing my days were numbered, that someone would betray me soon, I then travelled back to Scotland and the council of my men.

Big Duncan attended this meeting and put a plan to me which could very well have toppled the English crown. We would swap places; he would become William Wallace while I would travel back to France in a bid for support from King Philip IV. Upon my return with the forces of France behind me, Scotland could then invade England once again, only this time we would have the power to be able to crush King Edward I's forces.

Acting as my body double Big Duncan was captured by the English and tried at Westminster Abbey where he was sentenced to death. On August 23rd 1305 I watched from the crowds as my doppelganger was tortured and beheaded. His body was hacked up, his head was boiled and set on London Bridge and his quartered body was sent to Newcastle, Berwick, Stirling and Perth as a warning to anyone who dared defy the English King.

With William Wallace dead I had a decision to make. Would I reprise my role as Scottish warrior and continue to fight, to inspire my countrymen into fighting for Scotland by returning from the dead, or would I walk away. Over the years I believe I made the right decision, with Sir William Wallace dead he became more than a single man, he became a folk hero, a legend, an identity for my home country, he became the embodiment of the Scottish people, much more than I could have ever been.

And so I left, heading South through France, onto Spain and then down to Morocco, always searching for others like me, others able to survive the sword. For three centuries I travelled the known world, following local myths and legends to try and find their origins, to try and find others. This search found me back in Scotland on the trail of an old woman born before any other could remember. It was rumoured the Crawford Witch lived out in the forests surrounding Loch Trool in Galloway. I can recall as clear as this morning's breakfast my encounter with the witch who had lived longer than any other.

It was a bright morning in spring. I had made camp for the night with my horse and cart and planned journeying into the forest that very morning to find the fabled immortal witch. I had been awake for perhaps half an hour when my horse stirred, pulling at his reins which secured him to the cart. As I moved around the cart to see what the trouble was she appeared from the trees, hair shining silver in the morning light and in her hand she held what I now know to be a Japanese samurai sword.

I lifted up my hand in greeting and she returned the courtesy with a flick of the katana blade.

'You are not welcome here,' she told me, speeding up her movement as we approached each other, 'leave now.'

I held up my hands, 'I mean you no harm,' I told her as her face became clearer. She then stopped and gasped, the sword falling to the earth and her to her knees.

'William? No, it cannot be. William?'

I stopped, now wary of the name I had not used in over a century. I reached for my own sword, the heavy metal in my hand reassuring.

'You are the witch Crawford are you not? I come to speak to you of things of a magical essence.'

The old lady was slumped over onto her elbows and was sobbing uncontrollably. This hadn't been the start to the meeting I had envisioned.

'You come to speak to me of magic,' she said, getting up onto her knees, her skin although aged, still had the colour of youth about it, making the old lady appear as though she was a much younger woman dressing up as an old one. 'Tell me Sir William Wallace, in the three hundred and two years since your execution is it magic which brings you to me now?'

I gazed into her pale blue eyes, and the glimpse of recognition stirred something inside me.

'Who are you? How is it you know of me?'

'I was just a young girl when you left to fight and you never came back for me. You left without sparing me a second thought.'

'Nessie?'

My little sister smiled and then stood up off the ground, and it was at that moment, as she walked towards me with her arms held out for me that I could see the little girl whom I had promised I would not desert. In our embrace I dropped to my knees and kissed the wrinkled hand which belonged to my little sister.

'I don't understand, how is it you did not die many years ago?'

Picking myself back up we walked back towards my cart and Nessie said, 'I did die, in my fifty second year I fell ill with a great cough. I then fell into a deep sleep and when I woke my family had me laid out in my best dress ready for burial. I had returned from the dead and the town in which I had lived for thirty years turned against me. I was captured and tortured, burned at the stake and then my charred body was dumped into a casket and thrown into a swamp. My body healed and I made my way to the surface, realising there was no point in going back and so, like you, I moved away.'

I nodded to her sword, 'That is an interesting shaped sword.'

'It's Japanese, dear brother, the Katana sword. I moved far enough away so that the stories of my rising from the dead did not follow.'

'Why did you come back?'

Nessie shrugged at this, 'Scotland is my home, and after sixty years my story is now third generation. Any woman old enough to remember my face is now long dead and buried. These days any old lady past the age of sixty is witch Crawford,' she smiled.

We stopped at my cart and I took Nessie's hand in mine, 'I am so happy to see you. I have felt so alone for all these years, not knowing if I was the only one with this amazing gift, and now I find you.'

Nessie smiled again, the little girl I remembered so well shining through in that smile.

'Oh William, you must stay with me, there is so much we have to talk about.'

I nodded at this, 'Of course, first let me make the trip into the next town so that I might buy provisions for my stay. I will spare no expense. Tonight we will dine on roasted Pheasant and potatoes and wash it down with the finest mead I can purchase. Tell me dear Nessie, where is your home so that I might find it upon my return?'

Nessie pointed at the trees, 'a ten minute walk up that ridge lays Loch Trool. On the far side of the loch there is a path which winds into the forest. Follow that path and you will eventually arrive at the wicked witch Crawford's evil cabin.'

'Sounds enchanting,' I told her as I saddled my horse, 'I will see you in a few hours.'

She waved me off down the road and when I returned that evening she would ambush me, locking me in the Iron box I called home for forty years. The year was 1607 and Nessie was the first of my kind I ever came into contact with.

Chapter Fifteen

ABILITIES

'It is wonderful to meet you sir,' Mr. Macmillan says, grasping my hand and shaking it enthusiastically.

'Alright Bertie, you'll take his bloody arm off,' Eric says as he sits down on the edge of his desk and nods for me to take a seat on the sofa. Apinya stands in the corner by the fireplace and Mr. Macmillan sits down in a chair to my left.

'For years I've been asking Eric to give up your name so I might arrange to meet you, attempting it would seem to change future events as you will add this meeting into your book. I'm honoured sir.'

'Honoured, you hear Doc?' Eric says. ' At least now

you'll stop bugging me. I swear, he'll be asking for your autograph before we leave.'

'Leave? I'm struggling to understand how I *arrived* here. What is this place Eric? Apinya?'

Eric jumps down off the corner of his desk and picks a book from the bookshelf to his right, admiring the leather-bound cover and then throwing it across the room to me.

I catch it, spinning it around in my hands. Immortal - *a memoir* is the title embossed into the leather.

Opening the cover I read the dedication and smile, aware that now I have read it this is what I will write when my time comes to dedicating my memoir. I flick through a couple of pages and land on the Prologue, A New Dawn, the very chapter I wrote just a few days ago. Closing the book up again I turn to Apinya and ask, 'Can I take this with me? It'd certainly be easier to just copy it word for word.'

Apinya shakes his head, 'If only life was that easy William, but there is no taking it anywhere, we are still sat in your cottage.'

I feel the frown forming on my brow. What does he mean? We are here, somehow, at Chesterfield Manor.

'How did I get here?' I ask.

My new friend Mr. Macmillan or Bertie, as Eric calls him, waves a hand, 'We'll deal with the how in a moment. The why is more important. You're here because we've gathered to tell you about a world, a world you will head towards after the publication of your book.'

Eric steps forward, 'Right now you are lost, isn't that right William? You strive to find more of the immortal, your Divine. Teaching job after teaching job, each war that arises you reluctantly enlist, hoping as you did with me, to find others, men and women who time does not touch. I know this, you have told me this many times through the years.'

I nod. He's right. Always my sounding board, always there to listen to my frustrations.

'That's why I thought about penning a memoir. This one here it would seem,' I say, holding up the book, my finished works.

'It will be published at the end of this year, and it will go on to become extremely successful. So much so that the book will spark a following, people who love the idea of it being true. Imagine being able to live forever. For the mortal man he paints a fantasy in his mind aided by your words. More than that though, the book will eventually find its readership, the Divine, and we will be united in a sense.'

'We'll go public?' I ask, searching the faces of each of the men in front of me.

Eric turns to Apinya, eyebrows arched, asking him if this is so. The time traveller who takes short cuts up and down the centuries, shakes his head and says, 'No. When I am from there is unrest. Hints on social media and the internet of the Divine existing, but they have not gone public…yet.'

'Sorry, I feel like an idiot but what is social media and the internet?'

Mr. Macmillan bursts out laughing, 'Oh William let me tell you, the amount of times I've felt like this when arriving here with Eric standing over me knowing everything and me knowing nothing…social media and the internet are to all extent and purposes forms of communication. Like a newspaper but a little wider.'

I watch as Eric and Apinya smile at this description of future technologies I have yet to live through.

'And you say they, but you too are Divine are you not?' I ask Apinya.

'Not yet,' he says, 'I have yet to test out your Divine gene, I have yet to die.'

'And you,' I ask the man sat in front of me, 'You are like me, like Eric?'

Mr. Macmillan holds up his hands in surrender, 'Guilty as charged William.'

'Do you have any other abilities other than longevity?'

He nods, 'Yes I do. I am able to create subconscious planes on which I can guide the recently departed back to their most cherished memory so that they might spend their eternity there.'

I nod, 'Just so I'm not confused, what the hell does that even mean?'

Eric's Bertie grins, 'I'm a guardian of the afterlife… and up until recently, I was also a hospital porter in one of the five hundred hospitals I owned. A man still needs to do a day's work after all.'

'Of course,' I agree, shaking my head and picking the book up again.

'Why did you bring me here, Apinya?'

Apinya shakes his head, 'Because you need to see this place, understand where we are so that you might write about it and also because you taught me so much as a child William, you really were my mentor, a time yet to come for you. I want you to understand the nature of this place and to answer the question you asked me before I brought you here.'

'This place, this office, the rolling hills you see through the window, the oak tree you woke up under, is all projection, an idea, a memory of the host's,' Eric says. 'Like Bertie, I too am able to reach out to others, invite them inside my head, I guess.'

I nod, flicking through the book again.

'I brought you here William because…'

'Yes, yes, I know, because you always did. That there isn't a version of events which this trip into the future didn't happen.'

'Rude,' Apinya smirks.

'Tell me about it,' Eric replies. 'You were only trying to explain the why to him.'

They both snigger amongst themselves and I laugh, 'Alright, very good, this is all a big joke which I am not privy to. Please, both of you, just stop for a moment will you?'

They both nod and I once again flick through the very memoir I am struggling to find the words for back in the present, my present. I flick close to the end and read the title God Or Monster. This is something I have always wondered about our kind, The Divine. Are we Divine? Have we been touched by a great creator, or are we a mutated abomination of Man? I have no answers, I can only ask questions and in doing so, in writing those questions down, telling my story, perhaps it will reach others with questions of their own.

I look up at Mr. Macmillan and smile, 'Robert, have you met many Divine in your years?'

He shakes his head, 'Not many no, and I guess I am in the perfect place to find them. I tend to the elderly and the terminally ill William, those who do not have long to go. If one of my patients was to die and then reanimate, I'd know about it.'

'Talk me through what happens, how you connect with the dead.'

Mr. Macmillan leans forward in his chair, clearing his throat and smiling again, 'I feel a buzzing in my head. Sometimes it is only faint and I don't even notice until a patient walks up to me and starts talking. Other times that buzzing is like a crack of thunder inside my mind and I know somewhere close someone is passing over.'

'So it is their plane of thought? The patients? If you don't even know they're there sometimes, how could it be you?'

'I think it is subconscious to a certain degree. This ability I have, this place my mind creates, it is familiar to the patient. I paint a picture in my mind of the hospital and when they die they feel as though they've just left their room and see me standing there alone in the corridor. We will talk and we walk, them always talking about their favourite memory. When it happens in the hospital I lead us to the elevator and they push a button. When the door opens they step out into that memory as the person they were back then.'

'So they change in appearance?'

He nods, 'William, it is all projection. Just as I project the hospital corridor and elevator, their memories project what is on the other side of that door. Yes their appearance changes but again, they left their failed body in their hospital bed.'

'How many times has this happened to you?'

'How many? Hundreds of times. I dare say if I didn't hang around the dying on a day to day basis the number would be far fewer, but this is who I am. Like I said, I'm the guardian.'

So many ideas, so many questions. I always knew there was more to us than just our inability to stop breathing. My strength, Eric's flight and invisibility, Apinya's ability to travel through time, and now Mr. Macmillan, the angel of death.

I look up at the boy, 'Apinya, before you brought me here I asked you a question, I wanted to know how you disarmed that thug on the car park simply by touching him.'

'I have the ability to suck the life force out of any living thing,' he says, and then, 'I am also able to heal.'

'Heal? Like…heal?' I repeat, smiling.

'Exactly like that, yes.'

'But how?'

'You're the Doc,' Eric says, 'It is up to you to figure it out, and I'm sure you will, in time, that one thing we have in abundance. For now though Apinya felt you needed a kick up the arse. Tell your story William, talk about your life. This is *your* memoir after all. Just write it.'

I stand up from my seat and hold out my hand which Mr. Macmillan takes, shaking it firmly and telling me how wonderful it was to finally meet me.

'I'm ready,' I tell Apinya and as he moves forward I turn to Eric, 'See you next time brother. No doubt you'll have a giggle with me about this meeting.'

'No doubt,' Eric beams, and we hug each other, 'Stay safe Doc, and start putting pen to paper.'

I nod and as Apinya places his hand on my shoulder I feel a jerk, like when you fall in your sleep. I open my eyes and as promised, we are still in my faculty cottage. I am leaning over Apinya's mug about to pour him a second helping of whiskey.

'Welcome back,' he says, and then, 'Make this one a double.'

Chapter Sixteen

WITCHES AND WIZARDS

Salem, Massachusetts 1692. The infamous Witch Trials started in February 1692 and continued until May 1693. I was there and I watched the hangings of the innocent men and women thought by those in power to be witches and wizards, to possess some sort of magical power. Those who perished did so because of mass hysteria. Those who did not follow the rules, attend Church, raise a family, live as others did, were scorned and thought to have interests elsewhere, namely with the devil. In this day and age it is almost laughable to think communities feared these accused of witchcraft, but back then minds were small and the word of your priest or politician was gospel.

Whispers of witches in Salem and neighbouring towns had taken me there. Like the feared Crawford Witch in Scotland had resulted in me reacquainting myself with my sister who I had believed to be long dead, I thought there had to be some truth to the hysteria. There had to be the Divine living amongst the people of Massachusetts. I did not believe these rumours and accusations could be completely unfounded. There is always an element of truth in every lie.

My hopes of finding another one of us yielded little result. People were afraid of new faces, suspicious of anyone asking questions about the Witch Trials, as if to even speak of it might bring a curse upon them and their families. There was one man, an elderly former councilman, late into retirement and even further into what we now know as dementia, who described meeting the real witch of Salem as she passed through rural Massachusetts, travelling South to Florida. She had made her way to the Americas from Italy he claimed, although her English had been flawless and she had boasted being fluent in many languages.

Pressing the elderly councilman, he revealed the young lady had told him she had lived for many years and in many countries. She had been present during the fall of Constantinople in 1453, witnessed the beheading of half a dozen kings and queens as she travelled throughout Europe and the Americas. I tried to question why this woman, the Salem Witch, would offer her story so freely but the elderly councilman could not say. His mind was deteriorating and I felt I could not trust the man's story in its entirety.

But what if she had been real and said these things to this man? Providing this woman had not also been beheaded, there is a very real chance she is alive today. I hope she is, and I hope she is happy. I often wonder, as I do with all of my brothers and sisters, if they too are searching for more of us. The Salem Witch who was burnt at the stake, drowned, flogged, and much more…is she out there somewhere? Does she have a family and is she happier in these more tolerant times? I hope so. I hope this Salem Witch who had left town long before the trials began has found peace, although it is hard to know you are different from the others around you and not ask why. We are not witches, nor wizards, angels or demons. We are another species, the Orang-Utans to man's Gorilla, so close in our DNA, cousins, but the differences are those which allow us our longevity, allows me my strength and allows the Salem Witch, if one is to believe a demented councilman, the ability to read minds and enchant inanimate objects. It is also this shift of our DNA which would allow a young boy the ability to travel through time through his subconscious.

In writing this, the year is 1958 and I have met the time travelling boy twice in my life. The first time he is to meet me will be in 2003, I am told he will be scared, confused, and in a foreign land, and I will help him master his abilities. The first time I met him was in 1916, and it was only when the young boy showed up once again that I understood who he was…what he was.

Chapter Seventeen

TIME, DEATH, LOVE

He is the guardian of time. I understand that now. Three forces, none of which can ever be adequately explained, had invited me to Chesterfield Manor. Time, Death and Love. These entities visit us all throughout our lives. For the moment we are conceived, time is our companion through this crazy journey called life. We cannot escape it, it is a constant until we meet our end. Time is magical. A moment's embrace in the arms of love can last an eternity and yet be over all too soon. Equally, a minute of boredom might feel to last quite a different eternity all together. Time is not real and yet it governs our whole lives. In each moment we are perpetually living in the present. Time does not move, it is us who move through it. Apinya has mastered a way to switch this dynamic around.

Time…the only way to stop it is death.

Humans have an interesting relationship with death. Some fear it, others celebrate it. Some believe another life awaits them after death, others see it as a void of nothingness. Whichever belief someone follows, Death is where Time has been taking us. There is no escaping it. Even I will one day die. I have no illusions that my immortality will last forever. I do not see myself still walking around in a million years time, I couldn't imagine anything worse. Everything meets its end one day.

Time and Death, the train track leading to the end of the line. It is what you do with your time while on that train which counts. This is where the equally mystifying Love comes into play. We all love and we have all been loved. To be *in* love, is perhaps the most magnificent feeling in life. It is a gift, that feeling, the chemical reactions in your body, the butterflies in your stomach, the euphoric high in your head. Love is the reason we live.

I have loved many through my years. I must admit,

the more lives I live the more selective I am about engaging in a relationship because I know that I must one day walk away from them. Because I cheat Time and avoid Death, Love is something I am only allowed to experience fleetingly. I will never grow old with my lover, never hold their hand as they take their last dying breath.

Time.

Death.

Love.

Apinya.

Mr. Macmillan.

And…Eric?

Could it be? Could my brother in arms, the once Vlad Tepes, the original vampire, really be the embodiment of love? Perhaps. It is true I do love this man, more than any other, and I have loved him for longer than any other, too.

Their little gathering has set me on course now. I know what I must write, and write I will, knowing that in time those who escape death like me will love this book, will know because of it they are not alone, that we are out there, The Divine…

. . .

I hear the knock at my door and before I might call out to query who is visiting me at this late hour, Apinya lets himself in, smiling and nodding at me sat at my desk, pen in hand poised over a piece of paper.

'I'd have thought you'd be using a typewriter.'

'No. I have one for the second draft, but this memoir feels as though it needs to be written by hand. There is a deeper connection between the author and the words this way…I feel anyway.'

He moves closer, leaning over me to try and read what I have written.'

'Oy, less of that thank you very much.'

'I just wanted a peek.'

'You've already read it.'

He shrugs, 'I don't know, it's like behind the scenes, watching the master at work.'

I laugh at this, getting up out of my seat, 'I'm not sure about master, but I will put my all into this memoir. Try and tell a story as well as fit six hundred and twelve years worth of life into the narrative.'

'I'm glad to see you're enjoying it,' Apinya says, staring at me for a few moments longer.

'What?' I ask.

'Nothing William, it's just that you have played such a massive part in my childhood. Eric too, sure, but you and I share this connection which I can't explain, I miss that version of you, my William, that's all.'

I pat the boy on the back, 'Give me a chance, I'll get there eventually. Tell me, after 2003, when is the next time we see each other?'

'For me? The First World War.'

'No, no, that's not what I meant. I mean when is the next time you see *your* William? The man who shares the memories of your childhood?'

Apinya pauses for a moment. He has his rules about telling me anything of my future and I didn't really expect an answer if I'm honest. He holds out his hand for me and we shake very formally.

'It has been good to see you William, but it's time for me to leave. There's a young lady I've promised to take out to dinner and I wouldn't want to be running late now would I?'

I nod, 'The guardian of Time running late?'

Apinya grins, 'The guardian of Time, I like that. Maybe I should wear a cape like Superman.'

'See you around son,' I tell him.

As he reaches the door he looks down at the dying potted plant on the windowsill and frowns, shaking his head. I then watch as he reaches down and lays a single finger upon a withered leaf. The leaf begins to twist, the crumpled brown turning into a life filled bright green. The tired limp stalk begins straightening, and then the rest of the leaves follow suit, flowers sprouting out of nowhere.

He turns back and grins, winking once and then leaving, my friend in time heading back to my unknown.

Chapter Eighteen

GOD OR MONSTER

Anonymity is our friend.

When I climbed out of my metal tomb in 1647 I made the decision to shun my anonymity and go public, tell the world who I was and what I was capable of in the hope of reaching out to more like me. I was under the illusion I could meet with men of power and explain my predicament and they would listen. They did not.

I travelled the world in the hope of being granted an audience with Kings and Emperors. My time in solitary had taught me patience but now I was becoming more and more impatient. People would not listen to me and if I showed my audiences what my body could survive I was either looked upon as a God or feared as a monster. Little there, I imagine, has changed if I was to reveal myself again now, in the twentieth century.

The human condition, I have come to believe, is fear. I have already written within these pages that man fears what he does not understand. He does not search for enlightenment, and in the masses man acts like sheep with their herd mentality.

Perhaps one day we will number enough to be able to walk out into the sun and show the world that we understand, that we know they are scared, but we do not have the answers, we are like them, asking the same basic question, what is our purpose?

Of course to ask that very question 'what is our purpose' is to go against everything I have come to believe. It begins hinting towards a belief in a grand design and if so there would be a designer. The universe is completely random, my scientific mind understands this. Chaos produced our world and every living thing in it, I know this, but even still I search for others to understand why when really there is no answer. We are because the world in which we live holds the perfect conditions to host life. Through time that life evolves or dies out, and again chaos dictates this. Perhaps I should abandon my search for others and in turn stop chasing our purpose in this ever changing always fluid world. From the moment we are born life is merely a fight for survival.

Those who follow whichever God they choose argue that there is a plan, that our time on this earth is a trial run or test for greater things to come once we die and float up to heaven on fluffy white clouds. The afterlife is our true calling provided we are good according to a set of rules written by men centuries ago blinded by their own faith in the almighty. If there was a God and we were welcomed into heaven once we died, what then? Do our souls spend their days sunbathing in the gardens sipping margaritas and being eternally happy? To me that sounds dull, and I would bore of the eternal happiness and eternal peace. Without pain there is no peace, without anguish there is no happiness. If being welcomed into the kingdom of heaven is our purpose then what then? Personally I feel sitting atop a cloud with the angels would become tedious, but what do I know?

My purpose in writing this memoir and scrapbook of ideas was always to try to reach out to those who might feel lost and need to know that there are others like them out there, but who am I kidding, I am just as lost as they are. I live my life as a man when I am something more, the great pretender lying his way through this very long and mostly eventless life. I need my brothers and sisters who are out there just as much as they might need me, more so even because I am the one attempting to contact them. I am a being lost in the dark and this book is a signal fire I am lighting so that others may find me. Perhaps there are communities of my kind already built, men and women from across history who are still here to this day sharing information and experiences and doing their utmost to protect our emerging species. I'd like to think so, I'd like to think that I will one day be welcomed into the bosom of a community of my kind and then maybe I will feel at peace, then maybe I will have found a place to call home, no longer a reject of time.

I feel my choice of name for our species maybe wrong. The word Divine signifies Godlikeness, and although as a younger man I did follow God, as a scientist I cannot afford to be so short sighted. As a man with the luxury of time I have devoted myself to knowledge, I have studied far greater than the ten thousand hours people say you must surpass to be an expert on any given subject, and still I am at a loss.

My friend in time once spoke of his theory of why we are here, that we were fallen angels cast down from the heavens and forced to spend an eternity walking the earth in Man's image. I do not think he believes this anymore, he is no fool, and where mortal man can spend his life shutting reason out from his mind, Eric has been on this earth too long not to see the emerging pattern.

Man is a savage beast. He seeks divinity in the way he lives his life, taking at will, killing those in his path to achieve great wealth and then fighting for more. Man is always striving to achieve more. More money, more land, more wives or mistresses, this selfish beast knows no bounds when it comes to living its life.

Every other living organism on the planet has its place and they seek to reproduce to ensure the survival of their species. For man this has become second to power, and religion plays a big part in this. Before religion man lived in small communities, hunted, fished, farmed, made love, had children, taught those children the way of the land so they too could feed their families when they grew. This was the circle of all life.

Man then stopped worshipping the earth which fed and sheltered him and looked up to the sky. He started worshipping the heavens above and the "divine" being which resided up there. Stories were constructed around this fallacy until the earth, which had provided for man and man's children, was lost to an all knowing, all seeing deity. Stories turned into legend and books were written, books which held the answers to all of life's questions. Still the earth provided man's nourishment and shelter but now man, convinced he would find eternal happiness after death, abused his provider. For the centuries that followed wars were fought in God's name. And still, to this day, if you look for the reason for the fighting across the globe, it is either in the name of whichever deity is being followed, or for wealth of some sort.

The fifth ape certainly has come a long way.

Maybe it is up to the sixth ape to bring peace and order back to the earth before it is too late. This, of course, would mean there was a plan in motion, and if so some sort of divine being would have had to create this plan.

I don't know, perhaps I have it all wrong. Perhaps we really are angels sent from the heavens to keep the human race in check. Some days I wish this was so. I would have a purpose, a calling, a reason for my immortality. Instead I continue to absorb as much knowledge as I can about everything, I learn different languages, I study genetics, and in a previous life I studied theology, once upon a time being a man of the cloth. I try and learn from a history I experienced first-hand to prepare for a future I sometimes fear.

Man is becoming more and more powerful. His wars are not fought with the sword anymore. I fear the future because I fear one day one man will press one button and that will be the end of us all.

In the year 1859 I picked up a book by an Author I was very sorry to have never met, for his theory changed my life and indeed how I imagined our place on this earth. I am writing my memoirs some ninety-nine years later and still I don't have it all worked out. I'm getting there, at least in theory, but I'm a long way off answering the big questions about how we came to be.

The book in question was On the Origin Of Species by Means of Natural Selection by Charles Darwin, and in it he talks about how life evolves, the strongest survive and over huge expanses of time mutate to fit into their changing surroundings. One of the examples he used in the book is the now infamous Galapagos Island Finches. These birds, almost identical to mainland Finches, had different beaks which had adapted to different food they ate. This mutation would have happened slowly through many generations until a new species was born, better able to feed themselves while their predecessors who had not developed new beaks to ease the hunt for food would have died out.

Is our species still in its infancy? Still running around with the lesser abled Finches but now better equipped for the hunt?

We are in many ways immortal, our bodies heal at a masterful speed and we do not age, or rather our cells do not make inferior copies of themselves causing the gradual break down of our bodies which we call the ageing process. Physically we are the fittest of any species which came before. This is our physical evolution but what about mentally?

I have experienced unexplainable blackouts through the years. I have developed memories I do not understand as I have not previously lived them. Might our whole thought process also have evolved or be evolving still?

I write this book to answer questions for you but I find myself asking more than answering. It is a never ending fight for the truth, for evidence to support my theories of us, The Divine. But is that not science in its entirety? Asking 'what if' to a whole manner of questions and then attempting to collect data, evidence to support that claim (what if)?

I have thought for great expanses of time about these blackouts and the memories I possess which make no sense, and I have another what if I would like to put to you.

What if, as well as conquering the physical world with our rapid cell regeneration and immortality, our minds have evolved to defend us from the outside extremities in order to survive or even communicate? Evolution is mutation, the corruption of cells which reproduce to form a longer, thinner beak so that particular Finch might be better equipped to hunt for food underneath the shoreline's soft earth as opposed to a squat more powerful beak used to hunt for food inland amongst the canopy.

Charles Darwin studied these birds for years, focusing on this one project, and was able to collect enough data to support his theories. This is something I lack, the data, others like me whom I might study to support my own theories. But I have time. That at least is on my side. Perhaps in a further ninety nine years enough of us will have come forward for me to be able to gather the evidence I seek.

I named us The Divine because without the evidence we are but a being belonging to fairy tales, a bogeyman to scare mankind if ever we were to be discovered. Always question everything. I do not believe we are Gods or monsters. I do not believe we are angels walking amongst men, but I do believe hidden somewhere in our bodies and minds is the key to this mystery of our own origin of a species.

PREORDER BOOK 5, RECKONING

Check Out The Series at **www.robradcliffe.com**

SIGN UP TO ROB RADCLIFFE'S READERS CLUB AND GET YOUR FREE COPIES OF ALL OF HIS SERIES STARTERS AND PREQUELS (2 NOVELS AND 2 SHORT STORIES) AS A THANK YOU

ROB RADCLIFFE'S READERS CLUB

Building a relationship with my readers is the very best thing about writing. I occasionally send out newsletters with details of new releases, special offers and other bits relating to my book serieseseseses…I really don't know when to stop with the eseseses…

And if you sign up to my mailing list I'll send you:

MESSIAH
The Divine Chronicles Prequel

Every generation forgets. He remembers them all.

When the Divine Gene awakens, the dead rise changed: unable to age, able to heal from any wound, and marked with extraordinary powers. They are immortal. They are cursed. They are Divine.

Across centuries and civilizations, their stories weave together, revealing that every myth, every legend, every age was real… and they are still here. The Divine Chronicles is a sweeping time travel fantasy series blending immortality, myth, and legend into one unforgettable saga.

UNLEASHED

Rob loves to rant, and then write it down and put those musings in silly little books.

Here he does just that, keeping it light hearted and very un-PC as he battles and rants about the ever changing world in which he lives in.

Never holding back, and always hoping to entertain, UNLEASHED covers his soul sappers (kids), and why Pets@Home refused to sell him a dog cage once they worked out it was actually for the children to "play in", indie-publishing, why parents should die early to give their kids a chance to enjoy their inheritance, and being single and approaching 40 in this digital age, as well as many more other day to day irritations.

THE RACE
Four guys, eight days, one Greek island...

Bradz, Greg, Stu and Phil all head out for some fun in the sun with a twist. The race has begun, the judge has donned his big curly white wig and the score-board has been drawn up. Now it's up to the contestants to battle it out between themselves for the greatest prize of all, the title of SEX GOD.

ONCE UPON A TIDE
Welcome to Lanndos

The Easternmost of the Stepping Stone islands off the coast of Athea. A place where the story will begin but not end in legends told.

This dark fantasy fairytale retelling series puts a unique spin on the tales we grew up reading.

You can get all of these books **for free** by going to **www.robradcliffe.com** and joining Rob Radcliffe's

Readers Club. There you will receive the occasional email letting you know about new releases Rob has on the horizon, plus you will have access to Rob's exclusive closed Facebook group Rob Radcliffe's Readers Lounge. You may unsubscribe at any time.

RECKONING, book 5 in The Divine Chronicles is available for preorder now!

Check it out here:
www.robradcliffe.com

If you enjoyed IMMORTAL enough to have finished it, why not think about leaving an honest review? You could also drop me an email at rob@robradcliffe.com, or say hi over on Facebook in my reader's lounge, I'd genuinely love to hear from you!

RECKONING ~ sneak preview

THE DIVINE CHRONICLES ~ BOOK FIVE

VICTOR: CHRISTMAS CHEER

The snow falls from the sky and I sit by the window, watching as the white blanket rids the city of its dirt and grime. New York's very soul being cleansed right in front of my eyes. From my penthouse view I take in the twinkling Christmas lights and cheerful demeanour of those down there on the street. Tomorrow it is Christmas day and all of those people below are busying themselves with last minute shopping, drinking with friends and colleagues in the bars and restaurants, and generally feeling that warm glow of hope inside them.

. . .

'Things aren't that bad, can't complain, at least we have our health, Merry Christmas!'

She doesn't knock when she opens the apartment door. I guess knocking is a formality which has long since passed.

'Are you going to join us for drinks in the restaurant downstairs?' she asks as she enters the lounge and finds me sat by the window.

I shake my head and wave her away, reaching for the bottle of brandy and pouring another measure into the goblet. In response, she switches the lights on and my view of the city skyline disappears. Her reflection behind me through the window now dominates and I turn and smile. She is wearing a new dress, maroon satin which hugs her figure. Despite our predisposition, Nessie likes to keep in shape and it is this shape which has kept me attracted to her over the years, over the centuries.

'You've cut your hair,' I say, taking a sip of my drink.

A shrug and a smile, 'Gotta keep with the times old man, do you like?' she asks, twirling on the spot dramatically and giggling.

She loves this time of year. For a couple of weeks at

the end of the year Nessie turns into an excited teenager, full of wonder, always planning her New Year Resolutions, and always buying me the most extravagant of gifts.

I nod, 'You look ravishing Ness, and have you coloured it as well?'

She nods, 'It hasn't really come out how I'd hoped but the lilac tint beats centuries of washed out grey.'

'It certainly does. You look twenty-five if a day,' I tell her, standing up and reaching for the arm she holds out for me. As our fingers entwine I spin her under my arm and we both laugh. I miss our dancing. In the twenties we always went dancing, but that was a different world, perhaps I was a different person.

We dance around the room for a few moments more before finishing with a kiss.

'Come on, we have lots to celebrate Victor. William and Niall are down there already, trying to out drink each other under the table on the Highland's finest whiskey…'

I snort, 'Bloody Scots at Christmas, you can take the boy out of Scotland…' I trail off.

'And I too am one of those Scots you turn your nose up at, just remember that. Down there in that bar are two of my clan's men, well Niall is originally from Ireland but we forgive him for that, and I would like to celebrate the festivities with both them and my man, you.'

I nod, 'I know Ness, I get it. It's a big deal that your brother William is back in your life, and I too am happy he is now on board, but I'm not one to be getting up in front of my employees and blasting out Mustang Sally on the karaoke while wearing a stupid red hat with white fur around the trim.'

'Scrooge.'

'Far from it little Scots lady.'

'Then prove it, come downstairs, have a drink with us. You booked the entire restaurant out for the night so that we could all kick back and relax. Join us please.'

Gazing into her pale grey eyes I find myself falling in love with her every time they connect with mine. This woman knows me better than anyone else in the world ever has, but she does not know the half of it.

'You know it is the wrong day you celebrate don't you? Christmas day, the birth of Christ, yeah sure that was allegedly December 25th, but it isn't the birth of Christ which people are out in their droves for. They are celebrating the festive cheer which is Father Christmas leaving gifts for children…and adults too.'

Her smile changes, tightens, humouring me.

'My darling, I am celebrating the array of whiskeys

behind the bar downstairs and I am also celebrating making it through another year in good health.'

She winks at me when she says this and forces a smile on my lips.

'December 6th, St Nicholas Day. That is who all these people are out celebrating, Saint Nicholas, the patron saint of children.'

'Modern day's Santa Claus, yes I am aware of who Saint Nick is, what I don't understand is why you are so mopey around this time of year. What do you care if Christmas has turned into the mass capitalistic spending spree where people go broke for the entire year just to be able to afford little Timmy that games console, and little Jessica her pink bike with glow in the dark handlebars?'

'I care Ness because I sit and watch the world turn into somewhere I don't much like to be. Christmas is the worst of it. That festive cheer, so fake, a moments gratification for a year of sacrifices. Man really is that stupid.'

'And what would you propose, banning Christmas? The very thought of it.'

I smile at her youth, her naiveté, and turn away, back to the window. Maybe I should tell her, explain to her that nothing lasts, everything is passing through on this journey called life. Admittedly some of us journey further but there is still an end. Just as in two weeks' time those decorative trees everyone was in awe of at the beginning of the festive season will be discarded and forgotten about, over time everything perishes after it's time shining for a blink of an eye. That is the nature of the world. That is nature.

Ness moves up behind me and wraps her arms around my waist. I can feel her warm breath on my ear as she whispers, 'What is it darling?'

I turn in her arms and kiss her hard, my love, how will she go on when I am gone.

'Nothing, sorry, yes of course I'll be down in a moment. Keep the party going until I arrive,' I tell her and she leaves, blowing me a kiss before disappearing out of the apartment.

I head to the bathroom and look hard at my reflection in the mirror. For millennia this face has followed me, unchanging, always the same, always constant, always here. I tilt my head forward and run my hands through my dark brown hair. It is longer than I usually wear it but my excuse is those winter months can be cold in New York. If I didn't live most of the year in Texas perhaps this excuse would be plausible. Letting my hair fall through my fingers I stop when the light catches an alien strand. I then pluck the offending hair follicle from my scalp and repeat the process to make sure none of those infectious follicles are left behind.

Six this time. Six grey hairs. Nothing much, nothing but my vanity effected having these hairs grow from my head. This would of course be true if not for the fact that in the two millenniums I have walked this earth I have not once had to deal with grey hair. I was thirty three years old when I died my first death, and when I came back I found my body could regenerate almost instantly. In two thousand years I have been shot, stabbed, crucified, hung, buried alive, burned alive, drowned and tortured, and each time I have survived. Now it appears old age might have been creeping up on me all along, playing the slow game, keeping in the shadows, waiting for the right moment to remind me that no man is immortal, not even the Divine.

COMING SOON. PREORDER FOR EARLY BIRD DISCOUNT!

Enjoy this book? You can make a big difference

Reviews are the most powerful tools in my arsenal when it comes to getting attention for my books. Much as I'd like to, I don't have the financial muscle of a New York publisher. I can't take out full page ads in the newspaper or put posters on the subway.

(not yet anyway).

But I do have something much more powerful and effective than that, and it's something those publishers would kill to get their hands on.

A committed and loyal bunch of readers.

Honest reviews of my books help bring them to the attention of other readers. If you've enjoyed this book I would be very grateful if you could spend just five minutes leaving a review (it can be as short as you like) on the book's sales page.

Thank you very much.

Author's Note

Hi there, I hope you enjoyed what has become a Divine Chronicles Prequel of sorts. Yes, there are a few chapters, or at least part of the chapters, which will have seemed familiar if you'd read the other books. That is something I can not help as this in a sense *is* the book, or at least part of the one described in previous books.

It's all very meta, I know.

It was great to bring back most of the ensemble from the series in bit parts, and also visit William at another part in his life.

So, how was it?

I don't ask that for praise, I genuinely ask this question because, although upon reading through the book during the second draft and believing the story holds up, my opinion is worth nothing. It is you, my reader, who needs to enjoy the scribbles. Yes, some of the book was taken from characters reading the book inside the book in previous…books (too many books in one sentence there) but I think if they weren't there it wouldn't be the book it was meant to be.

If you understand that, congratulations, I not sure I do, but never mind.

I have a few more DIVINE CHRONICLES stories coming your way soon so I guess I better get writing then.

I really do hope you enjoyed this tale and any mistakes you catch would of course be gratefully received, and I look forward to hearing from you.

I would like to also invite you to please leave a review, hell even a scribbled endorsement on the your local park bench would be great. That way I might reach and engage with more readers like yourself, prompted by your kind words (fingers crossed on the kind words).

Once again, thank you for your time, and I'll see you on the other side.

Rob Radcliffe

facebook.com/robradcliffefiction
tiktok.com/@robradcliffefantasy
youtube.com/@robradcliffe
instagram.com/robradcliffefiction
patreon.com/thereluctantwriter

Printed in Dunstable, United Kingdom